Praise for
Timmy Failure:
Mistakes Were Made

"*Timmy Failure* is a winner!"
—Jeff Kinney, author of *Diary of a Wimpy Kid*

"Will have readers in stitches."
—Lincoln Pierce, creator of the Big Nate series

"Seldom has failure been so likable—
or so funny."
—*The Wall Street Journal*

"Timmy is a terrible sleuth."
—*Publishers Weekly*

"Charmingly inept."
—*Parade*

Disney

TIMMY FAILURE

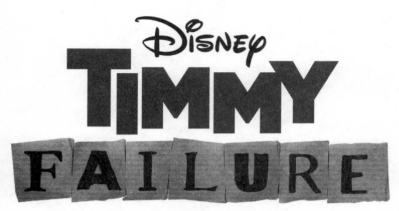

ZERO TO HERO

ZERO TO HERO

STEPHAN PASTIS

𝒟ɪsɴᴇʏ • HYPERION

Los Angeles   New York

First Edition, April 2020
10 9 8 7 6 5 4 3 2 1
FAC-020093-20052
Printed in the United States of America

This book is set in Nimrod/Fontspring

Library of Congress Cataloging-in-Publication Data on file
ISBN 978-1-368-06511-5
Reinforced binding

Visit www.DisneyBooks.com

Disney
TIMMY FAILURE
ZERO TO HERO

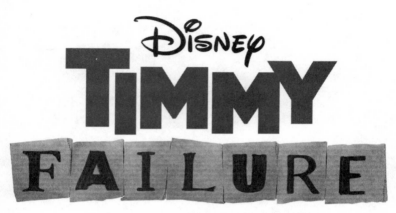

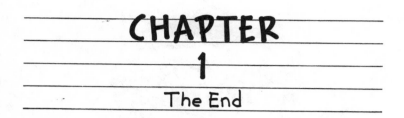

CHAPTER
1
The End

I have jam on my nose and a bomb in my hands.[1]

I found the bomb in a small leather bag in the back of a closet.

---

[1] It's a bowling ball.

While I was eating toast.

And the discovery startled me.

So I got jam on my nose.

But make no mistake.

The bomb is an attempt on my life.

And it was placed there by an assassin.

Because I am a detective.

A detective who has placed countless criminals in prison.

And I am so famous that there have been seven books written about my life.

And now a movie.

But the public's appetite for information about me is unending.

And so I have agreed to tell my story about how I came to be the greatest detective in the world.

Which I am hereby dictating to my best friend and biographer, Charles "Rollo" Tookus.[2]

But I have to talk quickly.

Because there is a ticking bomb in my hands.

And we are all going to die.[3]

---

[2] Me. The guy adding footnotes.
[3] We are not. Because it is a bowling ball.

CHAPTER 2

Temporary Diversion That Is Really Not Part of the Book, but the Book May Not Make Sense Without It, So Here We Go

(The following is a transcript of an argument between Timmy Failure, the subject of this book, and Rollo Tookus, his best friend and biographer. It is a shame to start a book this way. —Editors, Disney-Hyperion)

TIMMY: Hey, what's with the first chapter? It's filled with footnotes.

ROLLO: I want to be sure the book is accurate.

TIMMY: You're just supposed to write down what I say, not throw in your own two cents.

ROLLO: But some of it wasn't true.

TIMMY: What part isn't true?

ROLLO: Well, for one thing, the object in your hands is not a bomb. It's a bowling ball.

TIMMY: Wrong. It's a bomb *disguised* as a bowling ball.

ROLLO: It's just a bowling ball.

TIMMY: Rollo, do you think bombs have the word "BOMB" written on them?

ROLLO: No. But neither do they say "Manny's Bowling Emporium." And while we're at it, who titles the first chapter of a book "THE END"?

TIMMY: Someone whose life is about to be ended by a bomb.

ROLLO: Bowling ball.

TIMMY: You're fired.

ROLLO: Good. I have homework to do.

(Sound of items being shoved into a backpack.)

TIMMY: What are you doing with the laptop?

ROLLO: Taking it home. It's mine.

TIMMY: But how will I write this book?

ROLLO: No idea. But it's not my problem. Because I've been fired.

TIMMY: You misheard me.

ROLLO: Then what did you say?

TIMMY: "You're tired." Because you've been working very hard.

ROLLO: Fine. You know what? This whole thing is being recorded on my phone. So why don't we just listen to exactly what you said?

TIMMY: No.

ROLLO: Why not?

TIMMY: Because.

ROLLO: Because you know you said "fired."

TIMMY: Because I did not give consent to having my words recorded.

ROLLO: Yes, you did. So I'll just play the part where . . . (indecipherable)

(Sound of hands grabbing for the phone, followed by the sound of two boys wrestling, followed by the sound of a plate falling, followed by someone yelling "CHEESE SANDWICH.")

Recording ends.

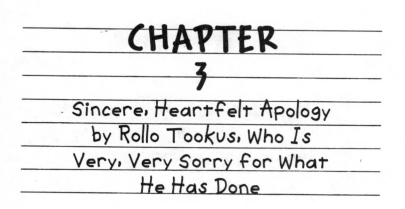

CHAPTER 3

Sincere, Heartfelt Apology by Rollo Tookus, Who *Is* Very, Very Sorry for What He Has Done

(Hi. This is Rollo. Timmy grabbed my laptop and wouldn't give it back unless I agreed to finish writing down this story, so now I'm writing it down, but I hope he hurries because I have an essay due in English that is one-quarter of my grade.)

(Also, I promised Timmy that from now on I would just write down everything he said and stop adding footnotes.)

(Also, I wish Timmy had another friend who owned a laptop.)

(Also, this is not an apology.)

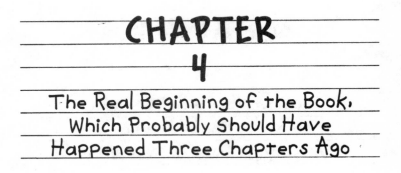

CHAPTER 4

The Real Beginning of the Book, Which Probably Should Have Happened Three Chapters Ago

In the beginning, there was a mother.

Who was visited in the hospital by a doctor.

"Ma'am, you are about to give birth to an extraordinary young man," said the doctor.

"Extraordinary how?" asked my mother.

"In all ways one can be extraordinary."

"That's a lot of ways," said my mother.

"Also, he is a genius," said the doctor.

"How do you know?" asked my mother.

"Because I have delivered many babies. But none like this."

And as he spoke, angels blew their trum-
pets. And the hospital room window flew open.
And in I flew upon a winged horse.

And I unloosed a scroll, upon which I had
written a lengthy introductory speech.

"Extraordinary," said the astonished doctor.

And I spoke for eleven hours.

And was beloved by all.

Okay, this is Rollo. And though I promised to not do any more footnotes, this is more of a note note, which I am tucking into the book.

Because I'm pretty sure Timmy was just born in a regular way. And there was no flying horse. And he couldn't read when he was one minute old. And I don't think the doctor ~~said~~ said anything, other than maybe, "It's a BOY."

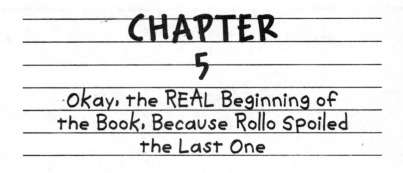

CHAPTER 5

Okay, the REAL Beginning of the Book, Because Rollo Spoiled the Last One

Fine. I have no idea what happened when I was born.

But it doesn't matter.

Because the person I have become was born the day I became a detective.

So let's just skip all the boring parts and head straight to that.

WHY ARE YOU
STARING AT ME?
GO THAT WAY.

CHAPTER
6
Spilling the Beans

"Mother," I announce, "I would like to be a burrito."

"Good for you," she replies. "Have a good life."

"For Halloween," I clarify, standing in the living room of our modest abode.

"Too much work," she says. "I'd have to make it, and I really don't have the time."

Which is technically true.

Because she holds two jobs.

And has held two jobs ever since my father left our house years ago.

"Fine," I answer. "Then we can keep the costume simple."

"Simple how?"

"No more than seven feet tall with thirty pounds of cheese."

ME AS
BURRITO

This part
all cheese.

"Timmy, are you nuts? Do you know how much thirty pounds of cheese would cost?"

"We won't eat it, Mother. We'll just shove it in the costume. And when we're done, we can sell it back to the grocery store."

"They are not going to buy used cheese," she says.

"Fine. Then how about a taco? Though I suspect its open design will create issues."

"Timmy, listen, I'm happy to take you to the store and buy you a costume. You can be a fireman, astronaut, cowboy, whatever."

I just stare at her. My eyes conveying the following opinion:

BORING   BORING   BORING

"Fine," she says. "Then I have an idea."

"If it's a tostada, it won't work. Those things are more open than a taco."

"It's not a tostada. It's better."

"What is it then?"

"Follow me."

"I don't even know what that is," I say to my mother, who is standing with me in the attic and holding up her "better" idea.

"Sherlock Holmes," she says.

"Who?"

"He was a famous detective."

"So he dressed like a loon?"

"Timmy, it was the style. He lived in England in the late 1800s."

"So why do you have it?"

"I wore it for Halloween when I was nine."

"I thought you said Sherlock Holmes was a he."

"He was," she answered. "But I wanted to be him anyway. What do you think?"

"I think it's worse than a burrito."

"Timmy, you're not going as a burrito."

"Well, I'm not going as that."

"Fine," she says, grabbing the box she got it from. "Then I'll just pack it back up."

But as she repacks the box, I see a shiny item at the bottom of it.

"What's that thing?"

"This?" she answers, holding up the object. "It's a pipe."

"You smoked a pipe when you were nine?"

"Timmy, it was part of the costume."

"Really?"

"What does it matter? You said you didn't want to be him."

I stare at the pipe.

"Can I at least see that?" I ask.

My mother hands me the pipe.

And I stare at myself in the attic mirror.

"It does seem rather distinguished," I admit.

"Timmy, he wasn't distinguished because he smoked a pipe. He was distinguished because he was brilliant."

"How brilliant?"

"Very."

"Did everyone else know that?"

"Of course."

I nod and glance back at my mother.

"You may have topped the burrito."

The coat is too hot. The magnifying glass is too heavy. And the hat is too big.

So I walk around on Halloween with a pumpkin and a pipe.

"Timmy," says my mom, "Nobody's going to know who you are with just a pipe."

"Of course they will," I answer. "I am a distinguished detective. And I am brilliant."

"Here," she says, putting the hat on my head. "At least wear the hat."

"It doesn't fit right."

"Yes, well, if you want them to know you are a distinguished detective, you need the hat."

So I wear it as we march up the walkway to the house across the street from ours.

And it slips down over my eyes.

And I fall off the porch.

"Well, what do we have here?" says the homeowner as he opens the front door and steps onto the porch.

"Probably a lawsuit," I answer from the bushes. "It appears your porch is defective."

"Hi, Bob," says my mother. "Timmy just tripped. His hat slipped over his eyes."

"*Your* hat," I correct my mother as she helps me back onto the porch. "And I believe I've broken my nutella."

"Patella," says the homeowner. "Nutella is something you put on your toast."

"Speaking of food," I answer, "I hereby advise you of the trick and the treat."

"I'm sorry?" answers the homeowner.

"It's how he says 'trick or treat,'" comments my mother.

"Mother, I don't need you to translate. I think you've caused more than enough damage already."

And as I say it, a girl emerges catlike from the house.

It is Toody Tululu, a classmate.

"Oh. Hi, Timmy."

"Good evening," I answer with great distin-guishment.[4]

---

[4] Sorry. I know I said I wouldn't say anything, but *distinguishment* is not a word. —Rollo

"What are you supposed to be?" she asks. "A chain-smoker?"

"Sherlock Holmes," interjects my mother. "He just doesn't want to wear the rest of the costume."

"It almost cost me my life," I inform her.

"Oh," says Toody. "I didn't know. Well, I have to go. Bye."

She goes back into the house.

"Hey, Timmy," says her father. "Did you get any candy?"

"Nobody offered me any," I answer. "Not even a meager pittance."

"Oh, well, it's just sort of help-yourself," says her father. "I left a bowl of it here on the porch." He looks around. "But it appears to be gone."

Gone.

Mysteriously.

As in the very type of mystery Sherlock Holmes himself would have endeavored to solve back in his hometown of France.[5]

What happened next will no doubt be the

---

[5] London, England. Also, France is not a town.

subject of countless biographies, scholarly papers, and doctoral theses.

SO HERE IS WHAT HAPPENED, RECOUNTED AS ACCURATELY AS POSSIBLE

A bright light shone down from the heavens.

And a divine chicken landed upon my head.

And the chicken saideth:

And the trees sang:

And the earth spoke:

And, divinely inspired, I pointed to the bushes with one mighty sweep of my arm.

"Your missing candy is right there."

And it was.[6]

---

[6] Because Timmy knocked it in there when he fell. —Rollo

And all who were present were shocked.

And amazed.

And Timmy Failure was born.

CHAPTER 9

Devil May Care, or She Might Not

"Hey, would you two like to come in for some hot chocolate?" asks Toody's father. "It's a bit cold out there tonight."

"Oh, I'm afraid we can't," says my mother. "I have to be at work early tomorrow. But thank you."

"Mother, these people want to celebrate my accomplishment. It would be ungracious to decline."

"Timmy," she says, "I have to be up early."

"If you want," says Toody's father to my mother, "I can walk him back to your house after."

"Thank you, sir," I tell him. "But it's just across the street. And are you even trained?"

"Trained?"

"Yes."

"Well, I'm trained in podiatry, if that counts," he says.

"And what is that?"

"I'm a foot doctor."

"I meant security. Are you trained in fending off assassins?"

"Uh, no."

"Then I shall walk myself. But if I stub my toe, I will phone."

I turn toward my mother.

"Don't wait up. I suspect the revelry may go late."

I enter the abode as my mother says goodbye to the podiatrist.

"I think everyone's in the living room," he

says as he closes the front door and walks up behind me. "Oh, goodness," he adds, "you have a huge rip in the back of your shirt."

I look at the rip. And it does not project distinguishment.[7]

"You must have torn it in the bushes," he says. "You know what? I have a son about your size. Hang on."

He departs from the foyer and returns with a T-shirt.

"We bought it for him on a trip through the South," he says. "But he never wears it. You're welcome to have it."

---

[7] Still not a word.

I put on the shirt. And see that I now look even more distinguished than before.

And when I enter the living room, I find the Timmy Celebration in full swing.

"Hello," I say.

"What are you doing here?" asks Toody.

"Your father invited me in."

Her father walks into the living room. "Timmy, can I get you some hot chocolate?"

I nod. "Thank you, Podiatrist."

"You can call me Bob."

"Thank you, Bob the Podiatrist."

I turn back toward Toody. "What are you doing?"

"Going through my candy from tonight," says Toody. "I'm trading with my friend."

The bathroom door opens. And I see her friend.

Who has jet-black hair.

And eyes that steal the soul.

And is the devil in disguise.

"Hello," I say.

"Hi," she answers. "Who are you?"

"Failure. Timmy Failure."

"My father invited him in," says Toody. "Timmy, this is Corrina Corrina. She goes to my church."

"Dressed like that?" I answer. "It's a wonder they let you in."

"It's just a costume," says Toody, who turns toward the devil. "Timmy goes to my school."

"Oh," says the devil.

"I plan on dropping out soon," I explain. "I think I've gotten as much out of it as I'm going to. Besides, I'm a professional detective now."

"Corrina Corrina reads detective novels," says Toody.

"I do too," I say.

"Which ones?" she asks.

"All of them," I answer.

"What's your favorite Sherlock Holmes?" asks the devil.

The podiatrist brings my hot chocolate.

"Thank you, Bob the Podiatrist."

"Just Bob," he says.

I turn back toward the devil. "So do you have a pitchfork with that costume?"

"I do," says the devil. "But you never answered my question."

"What were you asking?"

"I asked you what your favorite Sherlock Holmes story is."

"Oh, right," I say. "Gosh, there are so many."

"Yeah, but which one of them is your favorite?"

"I guess I'd have to say that really exciting one."

"Which one is that?"

"The one with the shark."

"What happens in it?"

"It's this story. And there's a shark."

"No, I know," she says. "But what happens in the story?"

"Oh," I answer. "Well, there's a clown. And he fights the shark."

"I've read every single Sherlock Holmes story three times," she says. "And I don't remember that one."

"Well, it's been nice meeting you," I answer as I rise to my feet.

"Are you leaving?" asks Toody.

"Yes," I say. "I'm afraid I've been enjoying this celebration so much that I lost track of time."

I walk toward the front door.

And pause.

And turn back around.

"Satan, I'm intrigued by your specialized knowledge in my chosen field."

"Her name is Corrina Corrina," says Toody, handing the devil an Abba-Zaba. "And I thought you were leaving."

"Would you be interested in a position in my agency?" I ask the devil.

"Do you want a bag of candy corn for that?" the devil asks Toody.

"I suspect that together we could dominate the detective field," I suggest.

"No," says Toody. "But I'll take that Snickers."

The devil hands her a Snickers.

"Don't feel compelled to answer tonight," I inform her. "But I will need your answer by this time tomorrow."

"I love Snickers, too," she says.

"I'll show myself out," I say.

CHAPTER
10
Pipe Dreams

"Timmy, you can't take a pipe to school," says my mother, putting bread in the toaster. "Halloween is over."

"But Mother, it's distinctive."

"Well, be distinctive in some other way," she says, taking the pipe from my mouth.

I go back to my room and change.

"Okay, where did you get that?" she asks.

"Gift from Bob the Podiatrist," I tell her. "Payment for my solving the candy case."

"I see. Well, it's better than a pipe, I suppose."

She hands me a piece of toast.

"And don't forget, I have that date tonight. So you have a babysitter."

"Who?"

"She's new. Her name is Wendy."

"Oh, goodness. She sounds terrible."

"You don't know anything about her."

"I can tell from her name alone. Wendys are omens of ill fortune."

"Enough, Timmy. What time will you be home? I'll make sure she's here before then."

"Probably midnight. I have to go to the city library."

"The library closes at nine," says my mother.

"Then I'll be home at nine."

"You'll be home at six. And since when do you go to the library after school?"

"It's top secret."

"I'm your mother."

"Mother, a C.I.A. agent entrusted with the nation's secrets is not given an exception for his mother."

"Fine, Timmy. But be home at six. Because if I find out from Wendy you were even one minute late, you're in trouble."

"Fine."

"Promise me."

"Mother, I'm a detective now. Our word is our bond."

"Then give me your word," she says.

"Word," I answer.

CHAPTER 11

In the Underbelly of the Beast

After school, I avoid open spaces and slink through the city alleyways to the library. For as a detective, I must always be wary of a potential ambush.

And as I walk, I stroll past a seedy bar.[8]

And I suddenly stop.

For to know a city, one must know its underbelly. And a darkened bar has lots of bellies.

---

[8] It is not a bar. It's a Starbucks.

So I kick open the double doors.

And, sidling up to the bar, I order a double whiskey.[9]

Though, for my liking, it's a bit warm.[10]

But I down it without complaint and sit at a back table to stealthily observe the criminals in their native element.

And I am immediately accosted.

"I was sitting there," says a man.

I look up and see a beast of a human. A man so large he blots out the sun and strains the floorboards.

---

[9] Hot chocolate.
[10] Because it's hot chocolate.

"Pardon me," he repeats. "But I was sitting there. I just got up to use the bathroom."

And just like that, I can see the situation has escalated.

So I stand and face the behemoth.

"I'm afraid this town's not big enough for the two of us," I tell him.

I scan his person for weaponry.

"I'm sorry?" he says.

I glance at the chair, knowing that at any point I may have to lift it and crack it over his oxlike head.

"I'll tell you what," he says.

I prepare for what he will say next, my hands at the ready on the chair.

"What if we share the table?" says the goliath. "Because I just want to finish my crossword puzzle."

He sits in the chair across from me.

It is a provocative act.

But I quickly realize that the man is worth more to me alive than dead.

"Fine," I accede.

"Okay," he says, grunting. "Now then. I need a four-letter word for 'hard substance.'"

So I engage.

"Muscle," I say.

"I don't think that fits," he answers.

"No, I am opening up a detective agency," I clarify. "Soon to be the world's largest. And I will need muscle."

"Good for you," he says, not looking up from his puzzle.

"Now, about pay," I continue.

"Seven-letter word for 'abundance,'" he mutters.

"Nothing," I say.

"That fits, but I don't think it's right."

"No," I tell him. "Your salary. I can pay you nothing."

"You can do what now?" he says, eyes fixed upon his folded newspaper.

"I can assure you of this," I declare, eyes fixed upon the horizon. "You will attain glory. Bushels of it."

I stand.

"Join me in something great," I proclaim, hand extended.

"Are you leaving?" he asks, shaking my hand.

"I'm afraid I must. I have research to do at the library."

"Oh?" he says, lowering the newspaper. "Research on what?"

"A variety of highly technical matters," I answer. "But I'm afraid you wouldn't understand. For we each have our strengths in life. Some of us mental. Some of us physical."

"I see," he says.

"And by that, I intend no offense."

"None taken," he answers. "But if you're looking for detective-related books, they're upstairs against the back wall."

"And how do you know that?"

"I'm the librarian."

Salon, Farewell

I return from the library with highly valuable intelligence.

Courtesy of my new colleague, Flo the Librarian.

Who, because of our bond, agreed to provide them for nothing.[11]

But the stack is too high.

And it impedes my vision.

And I accidentally walk into a foreign establishment.

"May I help you?" asks a woman with glasses.

"Where am I?" I ask.

"Maybe it would help if you put those down," she says.

---

[11] He got them for nothing because it's a public library.

So I set down the valuable intelligence I have gathered, placing myself between the books and the woman.

And I see toes drowning in water.

"Good God," I mutter. "What horrible act is happening here?"

"Pedicures," answers the woman with glasses.

"Is that legal?" I ask.

"Yes. I have a license."

"My apologies," I say. "I failed to see what this was at first."

"A hair and nail salon?" she answers.

"Right. Good cover. But I'm being serious."

"I am, too," she says.

"Are you C.I.A.? Or are you in collusion with the Russians?"

"We do hair and nails."

"Gotcha. Now is the toe thing a form of torture?"

"No," she says. "It's what we do here."

"But you're interrogating them."

"Interrogating them?"

"Grilling them for valuable intel."

"Well, they're telling me about their boyfriends, if that counts."

"Are you writing it down?"

"I am not."

"Of course," I say. "You have the place wired for sound."

The woman in glasses smiles. "Well, I'd love to chat more, but I have some customers to get back to."

"Do you mind if I listen in?" I ask.

"Sorry?" she answers.

But detectives do not ask twice.

So before she can say anything else, I barricade myself in a highly classified listening chamber.

But the intelligence is hard to make out.

And there is a great whooshing of air.

"That's a hair dryer," says the woman with glasses.

But of course that's not true.[12]

---

[12] It is true.

And I must not lose this opportunity to gain information.

But then I see a clock.

And realize I have lost much more than that.

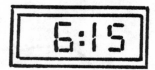

CHAPTER
13

Oh, Great, Another
Temporary Diversion.
Just What This Book Needs.

(The following is a transcript of yet another argument between Rollo Tookus and Timmy Failure, who at this point has just discovered the additional footnotes. We are deeply sorry.   —Editors, Disney-Hyperion)

TIMMY: Cad! Scalawag! Knave! Rogue! Miscreant! Chowderhead!

ROLLO: How do you not know what a hair dryer looks like?!

TIMMY: *(Indecipherable yelling)*

ROLLO: *(Indecipherable yelling)*

(Sound of someone falling off a chair.)

(Sound of fruit striking a wall.)

Recording ends.

CHAPTER 14

She Came in Through the Bathroom Door

I know I cannot risk coming home late.

And I am late.

But only one person can catch me.

And that is Wendy.

The new babysitter.

Whom I know nothing about.

Other than the fact that she will rat me out faster than a mob informant behind a witness-protection screen.

**TIMMY IS BAD.
VERY BAD.**

But I am a detective.

And I can outsmart her with detective logic.

Logic that dictates that a babysitter needs transportation.

But there is no car in the driveway.

And no moped.

And no bike.

So whoever she is, she is not yet at my house.

For she is not responsible.

So I strut into the house like a man pardoned from death row.

And spread schoolbooks across the surface of my desk.

So that when Wendy does arrive, she will see a young man pursuing his studies.

And I practice my greeting in the bathroom-door mirror.

"Oh, hello, Wendy. You're quite late. I'm sorry I didn't notice you. I was so lost in my studies."

And the bathroom door bursts open.

And I die.[13]

---

[13] He did not.

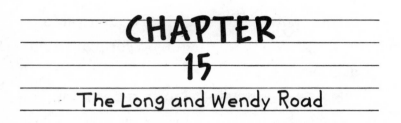

CHAPTER
15
The Long and Wendy Road

"You caused my heart to stop for eight minutes," I say to the babysitter who is now lounging comfortably on our couch.

"Doubtful," she answers. "That's a very long time."

"Your powers of stealth are admirable," I admit. "Were you trained by a foreign intelligence service?"

"No," she answers. "I'm in art school. You guys have any more chips? Your mom says I can have whatever's in the pantry."

I sit beside her on the couch.

"You may have heard I am founding my own detective agency."

"No chips?" she asks.

"I believe you can be an asset."

"Fine. I'll check myself."

I follow her into the kitchen.

"If I may ask, how did you conceal your vehicle?"

"What vehicle?" she answers as she rummages through our pantry like a starving demon.

"Your mode of transportation to our abode. I assume it's camouflaged by netting meant to mimic the average front yard of a middle-class home."

"I walked here," she says. "Oooh, corn chips."

She grabs the hefty bag of corn chips and I follow her back into the living room.

"Your skills can be very valuable," I tell her. "Let's talk compensation."

"Wait. What are we discussing now?" she says as she plops back down on the couch.

"Your pay."

"Is that any of your business?" she asks.

"Of course it is. I'll be writing the checks."

"Checks for what?" she asks.

"Salary. I'll be paying you to covertly enter homes, businesses, farms, county fairs. Obtain all the information you can. Then pass it on to me."

"Speaking of that," she says.

"Yes, tell me."

"Hang on."

She dials a number on our living room phone.

"If you're dialing Russia, I'm afraid I can't reimburse you."

She holds up one finger for me to be quiet. "Hi, this is Wendy," she says into the phone.

"You should really use a secret code name," I remind her. "These lines are not secure."

"Yeah, he's here now," she says into the phone.

"Whoa, whoa, whoa," I say, reaching for the phone. "What foreign agent wants to know my whereabouts?"

"What time?" she says into the phone. "Let me think."

"Who are you talking to?" I ask.

"Hang on a sec," she says into the receiver, then turns toward me. "Timmy, I'm trying to talk to your mom."

"DO NOT SHARE INFORMATION!" I yell as I dive for the phone.

"What was that, Ms. Failure?" she says. "I can't hear you."

"LOOSE LIPS SINK SHIPS!" I shout. "LOOSE LIPS SINK SHIPS!"

"I'm sorry, Ms. Failure. Hang on."

Wendy covers the receiver with one hand and whips her head toward me.

"Hush!" she says to me. "Seriously."

"BUT LOOSE LIPS SINK—"

She clamps her free hand over my mouth.

"Let's see," she says into the receiver. "I'd say Timmy got here about seven o'clock."

And kaboom.

The Timmy ship is sunk.

CHAPTER
16
Grounded Control to Major Tim

The betrayal by Wendy the Babysitter results in my being grounded for a full week.

A week that I have to go straight home from school and study.

And it is a week of delay that my detective agency cannot afford.

So instead of doing homework, I make productive use of the time by writing an agency recruitment letter to Corrina Corrina.

Dear Devil-in-Disguise,

As you may have heard, my agency has suffered a grievous setback. Caused by a double agent who goes by the name of Wendy.

Let this reinforce a lesson I'm sure we both already know.

<u>Never trust a Wendy.</u>
So while my agency is grounded, I thought it might be prudent to provide you with additional information ~~ about the job offer.

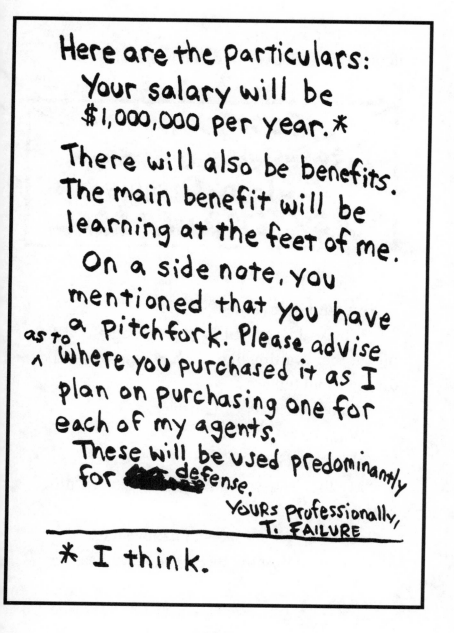

Here are the particulars:
   Your salary will be
   $1,000,000 per year.*

There will also be benefits.
The main benefit will be
learning at the feet of me.
   On a side note, you
mentioned that you have
as to a Pitchfork. Please advise
^ where you purchased it as I
plan on purchasing one for
each of my agents.
   These will be used predominantly
for ~~▔▔▔~~ defense.
                Yours professionally,
                   T. FAILURE

* I think.

The letter complete, I walk out the front door to hand-deliver it to Toody Tululu.

FOR TOODY,
Please pass on to the
Devil-in-Disguise
TOP SECRET-DO NOT READ

But I am intercepted.

"Where do you think you're going?" asks my mother, waiting like a covert assassin at the dining room table.

"Across the street," I answer.

"What for?"

I think quickly.

"My foot aches. Walking is now very difficult."

But I can tell she doesn't believe me.

So I begin limping like a peg-legged sailor.

"What are you talking about, Timmy?"

"If you must know, I believe I sprained it when the babysitter you hired leapt into the bathroom, causing me to spring into the air and land awkwardly. Perhaps you should have checked her references more carefully."

"First off," says my mother, "you were walking fine a minute ago. And secondly, what does any of this have to do with the house across the street?"

"I think the gentleman's a podunkatrist."

"Podiatrist."

"Well, I'm off," I answer. "Don't wait up."

My mother stands.

"Get back in your room right now," she says.

I sigh and walk back, my gait mysteriously cured.

"You're really harming the agency," I tell her.

"Too bad," she says. "Maybe next time you give me your word that you'll be home at a certain time, you'll keep it."

Foiled, I go back to my room.

Where I do the responsible thing.

Which is to use a rubber band to tie my message around a golf ball.

And open my window.

And hurl it at Toody's house.

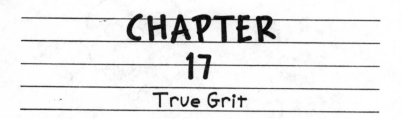

CHAPTER 17

True Grit

"Timmy broke my bedroom window," announces Toody Tululu to our entire P.E. class.

"She has no proof," I answer.

"He signed the note that was attached to it."

"Other than that, she has no proof," I answer.

"All right, pipe down, you little runts," shouts our P.E. teacher, Mr. Beefton, as he waddles into the gym.

OUR P.E.
TEACHER,
MR.
BEEFTON

"Timmy broke my bedroom window," she says to Mr. Beefton.

"Failure!" he barks at me.

"Sir, I have proof that I was overseas on business at the time and—"

"Shut your piehole," he says. "I don't care about a stupid window. I want to know why you don't have your gym clothes on."

"Sir?" I answer.

"Your gym clothes. We don't work out in street clothes."

"If I can explain, sir. I'm branding."

"You're what?"

"Branding, sir. Associating my detective agency with a distinctive logo, idea, or concept that I want the consumer to identify with me. In this case, grit."

"Grit?"

"Strength of will."

"Yeah, I know what 'grit' means. But your shirt says 'grits.'"

"Yes. That's plural for grit."

I am approached by the ever-irritating Rollo Tookus, who whispers into my ear.

"Timmy, grits are a food. Specifically, ground corn. Often boiled with water."

"Thank you, Mr. Dictionary," I whisper back to Rollo. "But I was trying to keep it simple for Mr. P.E. Teacher over there."

Who is not actually over there.

But over here.

As in next to my head.

"Get in that locker room and change your clothes right now. And when you come back, you're giving me ten chin-ups."

So I go to the locker room and change.

And when I return, Beefton points at the chin-up bar and tells me to get started.

So I do 160 chin-ups.[14]

And after I finish, I look at Beefton.

"Grits," I tell him.

The class erupts in prolonged applause.[15]

---

[14] Timmy did zero.
[15] No one applauded.

And when gym class is over, I return to the locker room.

Ready to once again brand myself.

With the shirt that is my trademark.

The shirt that is my logo.

The shirt that is not there.

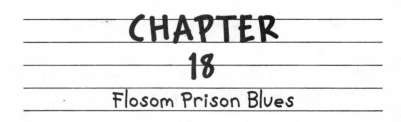

CHAPTER
18
Flosom Prison Blues

Facing an existential crisis, I run to the one person who can help me.

"Flo, I need intel. Lots of it."

He says nothing.

"Also, I need office space. For I have just been handed the biggest detective case of my young career. It involves a stolen shirt. I suspect we may be looking at a vast criminal conspiracy."

He says nothing.

"Here's what I'm thinking," I continue. "Your library has a kiddie section. It's fairly useless. You know, the area with the bunnies and teddy bears painted on the wall?"

THIS →

"Anyhow, I'm thinking we wall it off with huge chunks of concrete. Maybe some razor wire. That will be my headquarters."

He says nothing.

"Why aren't you talking?" I ask.

He clears his throat and glances up from his book. "You're allowed to take out three books at a time from this library," he says. "I gave you five, on the condition that you bring back the other two the next day."

He returns to his book. "You did not do that."

I immediately check in my backpack. But the books are not there.

"I am guilty," I admit.

"That was a personal favor," he says.

"Is there prison time involved?" I ask.

"Prison time?" he asks.

"Yes. A library jail."

"No," he says. "But if there was, I'd take every library patron who fails to push in their stupid chair and stick them in there for life."

"I will always push in my chair," I inform him.

He grunts his assent.

"Bring me those books," he adds. "Or you're not checking out any more."

I remain standing beside my colleague's desk.

He doesn't look up from his book.

"Why are you still standing there?" he mumbles.

"About that office space . . ."

"No," he says.

CHAPTER 19

Waxing Bare

With the Great Shirt Heist dominating the newspaper headlines, I have very little time for the missing books.[16]

But Flo is a valued colleague, and I have given him my word as a fellow professional that I would return the books.

And fortunately for me, I know just where I left them.

---

[16] The theft of Timmy's shirt was not in any newspaper.

"Can I help you?" asks a woman with scissors.

"Yes, I was just in here the other day and I left valuable intel."

"You left what?"

"Intel. Intelligence."

"I don't know what you're talking about," she says.

"Books. A large stack."

She turns to her other colleagues.

"Anybody see a bunch of books?" she asks.

They shake their heads.

"Sorry," she says.

"Maybe this would be easier if I could talk to the intelligence officer I was talking to the last time."

"Intelligence officer?"

"Yes. Glasses. Short black hair."

"That's Becky."

"Sure. If that's her code name."

"That's her name name."

"Great."

"Great what?"

"Let's get her."

"She's off on Tuesdays."

"What day's today?"

"Tuesday."

"I find that doubtful."

One of their confidential phones rings. Oddly, it is placed in open view of the public.

"I've got to get that," she says.

"Talk quietly," I advise her. "You never know who's listening."

As she walks off, I seize the opportunity to use one of their listening devices.

"Excuse me," says one of their agents. "Do you have an appointment?"

"I do not," I answer.

"Well, you can't sit there. The customer will be right back."

I smile.

"Listen," I tell her. "We can cut the charade. I'm an intelligence agent as well. More in the detective realm, but I have to interrogate targets just like you do."

Impressed, the agent just stares.

"Though I am not in favor of torturing the subject's toes," I add. "I think that's crossing an ethical line."

"I think you should probably leave," she says.

"Do not fear," I add. "For I will not report you."

And as I say it, I hear a cry from the back room.

"Good God," I declare. "What kind of operation is this?"

I run to the closed door at the back of the room and pound on it with my fist.

"This is Timmy Failure," I announce. "I am an officer of the law!"

"Hey!" yells the woman who had left me to answer the phone. "There's a customer in there."

"And they are in great pain!" I announce.

"She's getting her legs waxed!" she says.

"You have rights!" I yell as I continue pounding on the closed door.

Which suddenly opens.

Revealing another agent.

Who happens to be a polar bear.

CHAPTER 20

Mirror, Mirror, on the Scrawl

I rush to write a letter to Corrina Corrina.

> Dearest Devil in Disguise,
>
> Much to discuss.
>
> But since my last letter to you, I have learned that our correspondence is being read by others.
>
> Fortunately, I have been given access to highly-classified technology that will help.[17]
>
> So what follows will be in code.[18]
>
> Hopefully, you have access to code-breaking technology.[19]

---

[17] A computer and printer at the local library. Everyone can use it for fifteen minutes at a time.

[18] It is not. Timmy accidentally pressed "reverse image" on the printer, and he didn't know how to undo it.

[19] You just need a mirror.

Dearest Corrina Corrina (No need
for code names in confidential
communications),
    As you no doubt have heard, my
detective agency is growing rapidly.
It is already the best agency in
the state.
    As such, I have named it for
myself:
    Failure, Incorporated.
    I have also developed a mission
statement that is both bold and
comprehensive.
    Which is this:
    GRITS.

Finally, I see that you have not
yet formally accepted my employment
offer.
    As such, I am extending the
deadline by 24 hours.

I encourage you to accept the offer
as promptly as possible as I have
recently run into a particularly
appealing prospect.

I cannot disclose his identity, but
I will say that he is furry and weighs
1,500 pounds.

I am also in the process of moving
into office space that is both spacious
and prestigious.

I would happily share the
coordinates of said office, but as you
have not yet accepted said job offer, I
cannot disclose said coordinates for
said building.

Yours professionally,

T. Failure

P.S. I still have not received any
information from you regarding the
pitchforks. Please send.

CHAPTER
21
Office Space

"Your mom gave you the entire garage for an office?" asks Rollo Tookus.

"I believe so," I answer.

"What does that mean?"

"It means she did not object."

"Does she know about it?"

"No."

Rollo shakes his head.

"You're focusing on all the wrong things, Rollo Tookus. Focus instead on the massive amount of space I now have."

"Timmy, you shoved all your mom's stuff into a corner."

"Sacrifices were made," I tell him.

"I don't want to be here when she finds out."

"Rollo, she almost never comes in here. She parks her car on the street."

"Still," he says, shaking his head again.

"Listen, Rollo Tookus. I did not invite you over here so I could watch you panic. I invited you over to ask you for a favor."

"What's the favor?"

"I need you to give this message to Toody Tululu."

"Doesn't she live across the street or something?" Rollo asks.

"Affirmative."

"Then you give it to her."

"Rollo, I am currently grounded for matters I cannot discuss."

"Breaking Toody's window?"

"HUSH!" I say. "My mother does not know about that."

"She doesn't?"

"Negative."

"And you don't think Toody will tell her?"

I lower my voice. "Rollo, the whole matter is being handled professionally. You do not need to know the particulars."

"Well, there's one thing I do need to know," he says. "If this is for Toody, why is it addressed to 'The Devil-in-Disguise'?"

"It's a code name for an acquaintance of mine. Toody is passing it on to her."

"Who is it?"

"That cannot be divulged. It is highly classified."

"Oh, her name is 'Corrina Corrina.' I can see it through the envelope."

"OH, GOOD GOD!" I exclaim. "Rollo Tookus, you are the worst deliverer of classified information ever."

"Hey, wait a minute," says Rollo.

"What now?" I reply.

"This envelope was printed on a computer. You don't own a computer."

"So?"

"So how'd you get it printed?"

"After school at the city library. Now are you done asking questions?"

"I thought you said you were grounded."

"Rollo Tookus, are you doing me a favor or interrogating me?"

"Well, you said you were grounded."

I try very hard to remain calm. And count backward from ten.

When I am done, I walk toward him and whisper softly. "Rollo, my dear mother works. So she does not get home until six p.m. When I did those things after school, she did not see me. But she is currently home and in the living room, which has things known as windows. Have you ever seen one?"

"I have."

"Oh, good," I whisper. "So you're familiar

with the fact that one can often see through them?"

"I am."

"SO SHE WILL SEE ME CROSSING THE STREET AND I WILL BE GROUNDED FOR FORTY YEARS!" I yell.

Which startles my upstairs mother.

Who comes downstairs to the garage.

And startles us.

"WHAT HAPPENED TO MY GARAGE?"

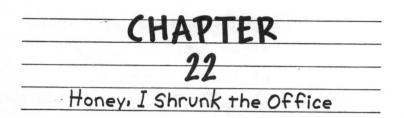

CHAPTER
22
Honey, I Shrunk the Office

The Great Garage Debacle was entirely the fault of Rollo Tookus.

For had he not asked so many questions, I would not have lost my temper.

And if I had not lost my temper, my mother would not have been alerted.

And had my mother not been alerted, my detective office would not now be relegated to a tiny little nook in the garage.

Sandwiched between boxes.

Though I have found enough room to display my mission statement.

However, this small space will in no way
house all the employees I plan on hiring.

And for that you can bla

*(Here, the manuscript for the book abruptly terminates.
Again, we apologize. If it's any consolation, we promise
to never work with Timmy Failure again.*

—Editors, Disney-Hyperion)

CHAPTER
23

Temporary Diversion That
We at Disney-Hyperion Cannot
Stop Because Timmy Failure
Is Out of Control

(The following is a transcript of the argument that occurred after the last chapter.)

ROLLO: None of what happened that day in the garage was my fault, Timmy.

TIMMY: Yes, it was.

ROLLO: No, it wasn't.

TIMMY: Yes, it was.

ROLLO: Okay, fine. Then I'll just go home and take my computer with me.

TIMMY: That's extortion.

ROLLO: I'm fine with that.

TIMMY: Rollo Tookus, that's highly unethical.

ROLLO: So?

TIMMY: So you wouldn't do that.

ROLLO: I would.

TIMMY: That's outrageous.

ROLLO: Then say it wasn't my fault.

TIMMY: Never.

ROLLO: Say it.

TIMMY: Rollo, I hope you realize that this entire conversation is being caught on tape.

ROLLO: So?

TIMMY: So extortion is a crime, Rollo. You'll spend the rest of your life in federal prison.

ROLLO: Say it, Timmy.

TIMMY: I will not.

ROLLO: Okay. Goodbye.

(Sound of person packing bags.)

TIMMY: It was all my fault!

ROLLO: See? That wasn't that hard.

TIMMY: So you'll stay?

ROLLO: No. I have to go home for my after-school snack. But I can come back after.

TIMMY: (Indecipherable)

ROLLO: Sorry. I'm hungry.

TIMMY: Will you at least leave the computer?

ROLLO: If you promise not to touch it.

TIMMY: I promise.

ROLLO: Pinky swear?

TIMMY: Pinky swear.

(Sound of door closing. Followed by sound of someone tapping slowly on laptop keyboard.)

ROLLO TOOKUS IS A BIG DUMB IDIOT.
ROLLO TOOKUS IS A BIG DUMB IDIOT.
ROLLO TOOKUS IS A BIG DUMB IDIOT.
ROLLO TOOKUS IS A BIG DUMB IDIOT.
ROLLO TOOKUS IS A BIG DUMB IDIOT.
ROLLO TOOKUS IS A BIG DUMB IDIOT.
ROLLO TOOKUS IS A BIG DUMB IDIOT.
ROLLO TOOKUS IS A BIG DUMB IDIOT.
ROLLO TOOKUS IS A BIG DUMB IDIOT.
ROLLO TOOKUS IS A BIG DUMB IDIOT.
ROLLO TOOKUS IS A BIG DUMB IDIOT.
ROLLO TOOKUS IS A BIG DUMB IDIOT.
ROLLO TOOKUS IS A BIG DUMB IDIOT.
ROLLO TOOKUS IS A BIG DUMB IDIOT.
ROLLO TOOKUS IS A BIG DUMB IDIOT.
ROLLO TOOKUS IS A BIG DUMB IDIOT.
ROLLO TOOKUS IS A BIG DUMB IDIOT.
ROLLO TOOKUS IS A BIG DUMB IDIOT.
ROLLO TOOKUS IS A BIG DUMB IDIOT.
ROLLO TOOKUS IS A BIG DUMB IDIOT.
ROLLO TOOKUS IS A BIG DUMB IDIOT.
ROLLO TOOKUS IS A BIG DUMB IDIOT.
ROLLO TOOKUS IS A BIG DUMB IDIOT.

ROLLO TOOKUS IS A BIG DUMB IDIOT.
ROLLO TOOKUS IS A BIG DUMB IDIOT.
ROLLO TOOKUS IS A BIG DUMB IDIOT.
ROLLO TOOKUS IS A BIG DUMB IDIOT.
ROLLO TOOKUS IS A BIG DUMB IDIOT.
ROLLO TOOKUS IS A BIG DUMB IDIOT.
ROLLO TOOKUS IS A BIG DUMB IDIOT.
ROLLO TOOKUS IS A BIG DUMB IDIOT.
ROLLO TOOKUS IS A BIG DUMB IDIOT.
ROLLO TOOKUS IS A BIG DUMB IDIOT.
ROLLO TOOKUS IS A BIG DUMB IDIOT.
ROLLO TOOKUS IS A BIG DUMB IDIOT.
ROLLO TOOKUS IS A BIG DUMB IDIOT.
ROLLO TOOKUS IS A BIG DUMB IDIOT.
ROLLO TOOKUS IS A BIG DUMB IDIOT.
ROLLO TOOKUS IS A BIG DUMB IDIOT.
ROLLO TOOKUS IS A BIG DUMB IDIOT.
ROLLO TOOKUS IS A BIG DUMB IDIOT.
ROLLO TOOKUS IS A BIG DUMB IDIOT.
ROLLO TOOKUS IS A BIG DUMB IDIOT.
ROLLO TOOKUS IS A BIG DUMB IDIOT.
ROLLO TOOKUS IS A BIG DUMB IDIOT.
ROLLO TOOKUS IS A BIG DUMB IDIOT.

ROLLO TOOKUS IS A BIG DUMB IDIOT.
ROLLO TOOKUS IS A BIG DUMB IDIOT.
ROLLO TOOKUS IS A BIG DUMB IDIOT.
ROLLO TOOKUS IS A BIG DUMB IDIOT.
ROLLO TOOKUS IS A BIG DUMB IDIOT.
ROLLO TOOKUS IS A BIG DUMB IDIOT.
ROLLO TOOKUS IS A BIG DUMB IDIOT.
ROLLO TOOKUS IS A BIG DUMB IDIOT.
ROLLO TOOKUS IS A BIG DUMB IDIOT.
ROLLO TOOKUS IS A BIG DUMB IDIOT.
ROLLO TOOKUS IS A BIG DUMB IDIOT.

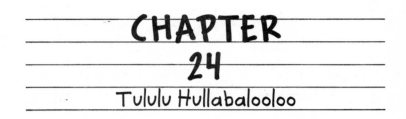

CHAPTER
24
Tululu Hullabalooloo

At school the next day, I am accosted on the playground by Toody Tululu.

"Hello, Timmy. Would you like to donate money to save the spotted owl?"

"Can't," I tell her. "I'm currently in the process of staffing my office. I do not have funds for said owls."

"Ten dollars should be enough," she says.

"I just told you no."

"Yes, I heard what you said."

"So why are we still talking about this?"

"Because I want to save the spotted owl."

"But I already gave you my answer."

"Yes, but they're so threatened. Especially with all these new homes invading their habitat."

"So?"

"So an owl might fly into a window."

"You are wasting my time," I tell her as I turn to walk away.

"I don't mean to," she answers. "It's just that the window could break."

I stop walking.

"Then I'd probably have to tell someone," she adds. "Like your mom."

I whip around.

"Toody Tululu, are you threatening to tell my mother I broke your window?"

"Nope," she says, smiling, "Just asking you for twenty dollars."

"You said ten."

"It just went up."

CHAPTER
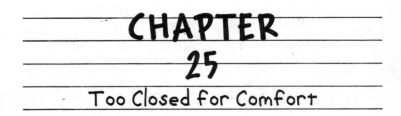
25
Too Closed for Comfort

My detective office budget has no funds set aside for extortion.

So I am forced to borrow the money from Rollo Tookus.

And after school, I meet Toody at the designated drop-off point.

"Why'd you want to meet here, Timmy? Is this where you get your nails done?"

"I will not be provoked by your absurd taunts. Let's do what we came here to do."

"Fine. Do you have the money?"

I take ten dollars out of my pocket.

"That's only ten," she says. "I said twenty."

"I know what you said. But right now I only have ten."

"Fine. Give it to me."

I hesitate.

"I will. But first say what you want it for."

"What do you mean?"

"What you're trying to do," I tell her again.

"Save the spotted owl."

"No, not that. Say why I'm giving it you."

"To save the spotted owl."

"No," I tell her. "Do I have to spell it all out? Say that I'm giving it to you because I'm being extorted."

"It's not extortion, Timmy. You broke our window. Either you give me money for the owls or you give it to my dad for the window."

"I deny that allegation. Now just say you're extorting me and make sure to say it loud so I can hear it above the traffic."

"Oh, fine," she says. "If that's the only way to get the money."

And grabbing my ten-dollar bill, she shouts, "I AM EXTORTING YOU FOR THE MONEY!"

"HA!" I tell her. "I have caught you in my trap! You are standing in front of an intelligence gathering facility that is wired for sound. Your words have just been recorded."

"By whom?" she asks.

"All of the hardworking agents here."

"Timmy," she says.

"Yes?"

"It's closed."

"Mind coming back and repeating all of this tomorrow?" I ask.

"I mind," she answers.

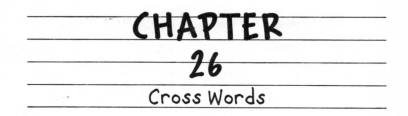

CHAPTER 26

Cross Words

Hemmed in by pressure on all sides, I stop by the local watering hole to cure my ills with a double whiskey.[20]

---

[20] Milk.

For while detectives work hard, they also play hard.

And nothing will get between a thirsty sleuth and his booze.

So I kick in the swinging doors.

And run into a beast of a man.

Which is too bad.

Because I didn't come here to talk about work.

And now I'll have to find another saloon.[21]

---

[21] Coffee shop.

So I leave the back way.

And there in the alley I spot a different kind of beast.

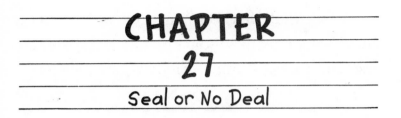

CHAPTER 27

Seal or No Deal

Now I should say here that you, the reader, will hear many different accounts of how I first met my polar bear, Total.

Some will say he wandered for food and found our cat dish. Or liked our cereal. And kicked in our back door to get some.

But those are lies.

Lies meant to obfuscate the truth.

And the truth is that when I first spotted him in the intelligence gathering site,[22] I recognized that he was a highly skilled covert agent.

Who was no doubt there on a mission.

A mission that required someone with a great deal of experience at extracting confessions.

---

[22] Hair and nail salon.

A fact that was confirmed when I brought him back to my headquarters and he presented me with the most impressive résumé I had ever seen.

NAME: TOTAL

Species: Polar Bear

Work Experience

2011-2013

Director, Central Intelligence Agency

2008-2011

Director, Federal Bureau of Investigation

2002-2008

Can't discuss.

Education

Doctorate, Harvard University, 2001

Graduated *Magna suppa duppa*

Skills

Assassin

Interests

Swing Dancing

After examining the résumé, I looked up at him.

"You are hired," I tell him. "I shall offer you a starting salary of $500,000 a year."

We shake hands.

And that's when he sees it.

The budget I have taped to the wall.

And he stomps out the door.

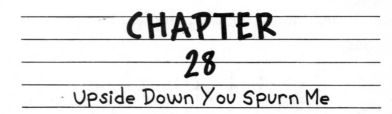

CHAPTER 28

Upside Down You Spurn Me

Dearest Devil in Disguise,

I write to inform you of major developments.

But security concerns persist.

As such, I am forced to once again write in top secret code.[23]

If decoding the message proves too difficult, please seek the help of espionage professionals, who should be able to provide you with detailed, step-by-step instructions.[24]

---

[23] It is upside down.
[24] Hold the book upside down.

Dearest Corrina,

I have not yet heard from you regarding my job offer.

To entice you further, I was going to offer you a more generous benefits package.

No, nothing boring like health care or dental care.

But a true benefit.

One that I was confident would be offered to you by no other Fortune 500 employer.

And it was this:

All the seal meat you can eat.

Unfortunately, I made the mistake of posting the offer on my office wall. And it was spotted by another recruit.

That recruit left my office in a fit of jealousy.

Which is a problem.

Because at Failure, Inc., we

strive to maintain a friendly work environment.

And the offer I was going to make to you caused great strife. Thus, I must regrettably withdraw it.

In addition, I was recently extorted for the sum of ten dollars, which has hurt our bottom line. As such, I must lower your $1,000,000 salary offer to $999,990.

Rest assured that all other conditions of your employment remain the same.

Yours professionally,
T. Failure

P.S. How do you sharpen your pitchforks?

CHAPTER 29

End of My Rope

At P.E. the next day, we are asked to climb a long rope hanging from the gym ceiling.

And as we wait in line to climb, I hand Toody the letter for Corrina.

"What's that?" she asks.

"You do not need to know," I advise her. "Please just pass it on to the intended recipient. And do not try to read it. It's written in code."

"Who am I supposed to give it to?"

"What do you mean who? You know who."

"It just says 'The Devil-in-Disguise.'"

"Toody Tululu, give it to the same person you've been giving all of the letters to."

"I haven't been giving them to anyone."

"What are you talking about?" I ask. "You're supposed to be giving them to your Corrina Corrina friend."

"Corrina? How do you know her?"

"I met her at your house! Halloween night!"

"Oh, right. Why do you call her the devil?"

"It's a code name. Now please pass them on to her ASAP!"

"Yeah, that's gonna be hard."

"What do you mean hard? You still see her, don't you?"

"Yes."

"So?"

"So I think I threw them out."

"YOU WHAT?" I exclaim.

"Tululu!" yells Mr. Beefton, our P.E. teacher. "Get your butt up this rope."

"I have to go," Toody says to me. "But listen, even if I still had the letters, I don't think I'd pass them on to her."

"Why not?"

"You really want to know?"

"Of course I want to know!"

"I think she thought you were weird."

"SLANDER!" I yell.

"TULULU!" Beefton yells. "I'm not gonna tell you again."

Toody grabs the rope with both arms and begins climbing like the dexterous feline she is.

"Hey, Timmy, one more thing," she says. "Rollo told me about you being grounded. Apparently, you can only go to school and back."

"So?"

"So you met me after school at the nail salon."

"What's your point, Toody?"

"So your mom would probably want to know that."

She begins climbing up the rope.

"You wouldn't," I say.

"I would," she answers.

CHAPTER 30

Cover Me

Surrounded by crises, I lie in bed that night to strategize.

"Hiding from someone?" asks my mother, peering her head into my room.

"The world," I answer.

"Ah," she says, "I know how that feels."

She sits on the edge of the bed.

"Why don't you read?" she suggests. "Didn't you check out a bunch of Sherlock Holmes books from the library?"

"Don't feel like it," I answer, not wanting to reveal that I can't find the books and may soon have a three-hundred-pound biker breaking down my bedroom door.

"Do you want to talk?" she asks.

"Not really."

"Okay."

"Wait," I say. "I would like to talk about something."

"What is it?"

"Can I borrow fifty dollars?"

"Fifty dollars? For what?"

I didn't think she would ask that. So I improvise with something credible.

"Seal meat," I answer. "I'm trying to recruit a new employee."

"I see," she says. "Let me think for a minute."

She thinks for no time at all.

"No," she says.

I shake my head. "I figured as much."

"So what are you hiring people for?" she asks. "Is this for your new detective agency?"

"Well, given that you're not on the board of directors, I technically can't disclose anything. But yes."

"I see," she says.

"It's very hard to hire quality employees."

"I imagine."

"And your grounding of me has not made recruiting any easier."

"Well, when you give me your word on something, you have to keep it. And anyways, I think your grounding is over tomorrow. Maybe

you and Wendy can go play mini golf or something."

"Wendy?"

"Your babysitter."

Wendy
the
Babysitter
(a.k.a. She who
rats on me.)

"Why's she coming over again?"

"To babysit."

"Mother, that woman has profound character flaws. She is not to be trusted."

"She's very nice."

"And why do I need a babysitter anyway?"

"Because I have another date with Philippe."

"Philippe? Who's Philippe?"

"Do you not listen to anything I say?"

"I listen selectively. To the things I want to hear."

"He's the guy I just went on a date with. He's fun."

"I don't like him," I say.

"You haven't met him."

"Instinct," I say.

"Oh, by the way," she adds. "He's a little paranoid about his car. Doesn't want anyone scratching it. So he asked if we'd mind if he parked it in our garage instead of on the street."

"OF COURSE I MIND!" I shout, waking our neighbors, the town folk, and the dead.

"Okay, calm down," she tells me. "It's temporary."

"HA," I retort.

"Sweetheart, he's just gonna leave his car here while the two of us walk to the movie theater. That's all. So I thought maybe we could just push some of the boxes to the side."

"But my office is in there!"

"Timmy, I did not give you permission to do any of that in the first place."

And I once again hide from the world.

"Are you not talking to me now?" she asks.

"Correct. Please go through my secretary."

"I'll tell you what," she adds. "How about I move the stuff for you?"

"Mother, my office was designed by a professional design firm with the assistance of law enforcement consultants.[25] You don't just 'move stuff around.'"

---

[25] False.

"Fine. Then we'll move stuff together."

"Wait a minute," I say. "I think I have a better idea."

"What is it?"

"Well, we're doing all this because you're dating this guy, right?"

"Right."

"Well, what if instead of moving the boxes, you abandon all hopes of ever having a social life?"

She declines.

CHAPTER
31
The Thing That Happens When My Mother and I Move the Boxes, but It's Not That Important, so You Can Skip It if You Want

The next day my mother and I are moving boxes and she is already asking deeply personal questions.

"Is that your school gym shirt?" she asks.

"It is," I answer. "If you must know, I had a favorite shirt of mine stolen from my gym locker. I have vowed to wear this one until said shirt is recovered."

"Why?"

"I find it to be a moving reminder of what was lost."

"Yeah, well, it's gross, Timmy. You're not gonna wear the same shirt every day."

"Mother, I have more than one gym shirt."

"How many do you have?"

"Three."[26]

She shakes her head.

"And by the way," I add, "you're welcome for helping you move these boxes."

"Thank you," she says.

"Now are we almost done? I have pressing matters to attend to."

"Yeah, just grab that last box and put it over here."

I stare at it.

---

[26] He has one.

"What is it?" I ask.

"It's just a box," she says.

I run my hand along its dusty top.

"But it says 'Tom.'"

"Yes," says my mom. "It's your dad's stuff."

"What's inside it?"

"Who knows?" she says. "I think he just forgot to take it when he left."

"Is he coming back to get it?"

She puts her hand on the back of my head.

"No, Timmy. Probably not."

"So why do you keep it?" I ask.

She just stares at me.

"I don't know," she answers.

She sits down on an old TV.

"Why don't we take a break?" she says. "I'm tired."

I continue staring at the box marked *Tom*.

"Come over here," she says.

I walk toward her. She pulls me onto her lap.

And we sit for a moment in silence.

"You doing okay?" she asks.

"Yeah, I'm not tired at all."

"I meant feelings-wise."

"Mother, I'm a detective. We don't have feel-ings."

"Well, that's good," she says.

I look up at her.

"I guess I am worried about one thing."

"You can tell me anything, sweetie."

I stare at the box.

"Do you suppose there's a live monkey in there?"

CHAPTER
32
Brief Interlude

(The following is a transcript of a discussion that occurred between Timmy and Rollo immediately after the dictation of the last chapter.   —Editors, Disney-Hyperion)

ROLLO: You sure you want that last chapter in here?

TIMMY: Because of the part about the monkey? It was a perfectly reasonable guess. He could have been a monkey smuggler.

ROLLO: I meant the part about your dad.

(A long silence.)

TIMMY: Yeah, I think so.

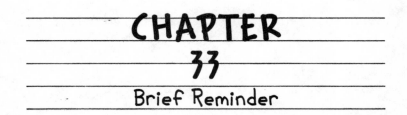

CHAPTER 33

Brief Reminder

Meanwhile, I am still holding that bomb.[27]

---

[27] Bowling ball.

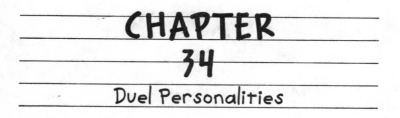

CHAPTER
34
Duel Personalities

Also, I met Philippe, a.k.a. my mother's boyfriend.

And we had a cordial, yet frank, exchange.

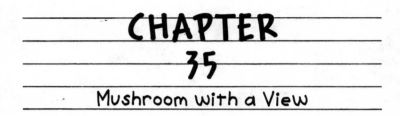

CHAPTER 35

Mushroom with a View

"You probably heard I lost my office," I tell Wendy the Babysitter. "So until I obtain a new one, this will be Failure, Inc.'s temporary head-quarters."

"I'm not sure the putt-putt place will allow it," answers Wendy.

"Why not? It's a perfectly good mushroom."

"Well, for one thing, people are trying to play miniature golf."

"Excuse me," says a man with two small children, "But do you mind if we play this hole?"

"Yes," I tell him. "Please find your own mushroom."

I turn back toward Wendy.

"People can be so intrusive. Now what was I saying?"

"That you need a new office."

"Ah, right."

"Why don't you just use your bedroom?"

"Not enough confidentiality. It's best to have no windows."

"What about your closet?"

"My room doesn't have one."

"Well, maybe you guys can remodel and add one," she says.

"Intriguing," I answer. "Oh, before I forget, you'll need to sign this."

"What is it?"

"A nondisclosure agreement," I tell her. "You violated detective code when you ratted me out last week. I can't risk a reoccurrence."

She examines the document.

"I realize it's filled with a great deal of technical language," I add. "So if you need help in understanding it, we could probably call my attorney."

"No, I think I can understand it."

"Also, you'll need to sign in ink," I tell her. "No using those stubby little golf pencils."

But before she can sign, a young man calls out to her from the batting cages.

"WENDY?"

"Oh, my God," she says. "That's my ex."

"Ex-what?" I say. "Ex-con? Did he do time?"

"Nick!" she calls out.

She runs over to greet him, leaving me alone in my mushroom.

Which is soon struck by a hard, spherical object.

It is some sort of attack. But fortunately, the

putt-putt establishment has provided me with a tool of defense.

I am soon surrounded by putt-putt authorities who ask me to leave the property.

And as I walk out the front door of the establishment, I see a grossly inappropriate display.

"Well, well, well," I tell my babysitter. "Canoodling with a convicted felon."

"I'm not a convicted felon," says the convicted felon.

"Timmy," she says. "What happened?"

"I deny everything," I answer.

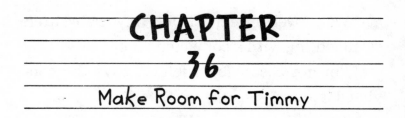

CHAPTER
36

Make Room for Timmy

When we get back to my home, Wendy raids our cupboards for cheese puffs.

"Mffthn," she says.

"Wendy, I cannot understand you with a handful of cheese puffs in your gullet."

She swallows her cheese puffs.

"Listen," she says, "I don't know what happened back there at the putt-putt course, but I'm guessing it wasn't good."

"Correct," I tell her. "You left me alone. I was attacked by toddlers."

She plops herself down on our couch and grabs another fistful of cheese puffs.

"Well, that's not what I heard," she says. "I heard the other people were just trying to play the putt-putt hole."

"You heard wrong," I answer. "But fear not. Unlike you, I shall not reveal a word of this grim episode."

"To who?"

"My mother. Nor will I mention the fact that I caught you in a love embrace with an unrepentant ex-con."

"Timmy, he's not an ex-con. He's an ex-boyfriend."

"Your story changes by the minute."

"Whatever," she says. "You want to watch TV with me?"

"I do not. I have office matters to attend to."

"Where?"

"In my bedroom."

"Can I trust you to be alone in the other room?"

"Of course. I will engage in no conduct that you have not already approved."

"I don't know what that means," she says. "But be good. We've had enough drama for the day."

"Grits," I answer.

"What's that mean?"

"It's my mission statement."

And as she watches TV, I walk down into the garage, grab what I need, and return to my bedroom.

Where I begin building my new closet.

CHAPTER
37
Mom and Punishment

"What were you thinking?" yells my mother after she returns home from her date and grounds me indefinitely.

"Mother, the babysitter approved everything."

"What are you talking about?"

"I told her I needed new office space. She suggested the closet in my room."

"Timmy, you don't have a closet!"

"Right. Which is why she suggested an add-on. So I thought I'd get the demolition work started."

"Oh, my God. I can't even believe we're having this discussion."

"Well, if you're going to blame someone, blame the babysitter. She's not to be trusted."

"Go to your room," she says. "Right now. Or I may ground you for the rest of your life."

"And here I tried to show initiative."

"NOW!" she yells.

So I go to my room.

And cover my head with the blanket.

And hear a knock.

Turn the page
for exclusive photos from

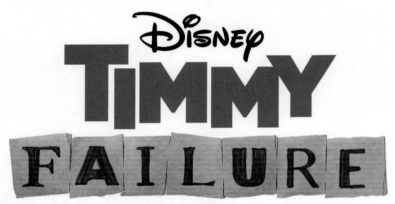

MISTAKES WERE MADE

Now on Disney+!

Timmy (Winslow Fegley) amends his Official Detective License.

Timmy's official business card.

Timmy rides the Failuremobile.

Ophelia Lovibond as Patty Failure.

Wallace Shawn as Mr. Crocus.

Timmy takes a quiz.

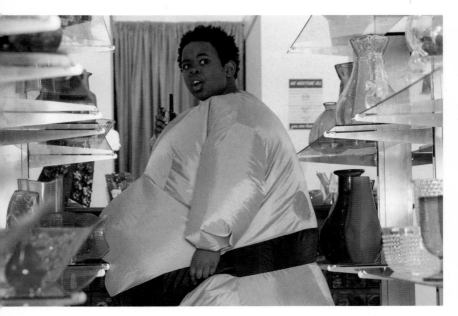

Kei as Rollo Tookus.

Operation Sumo.

Timmy questions Molly Maskins (Chloe Coleman) at the library.

Patty invites Crispin (Kyle Bornheimer) over for dinner.

Rollo and Timmy canvass the neighborhood.

Timmy and Rollo in disguise.

Timmy and Rollo on a top secret mission.

Molly Moskins at the animal awareness rally.

CHAPTER 38

Window to the Future

"You come at a particularly low moment for the agency," I tell the polar bear. "But it's all upward from here."

He brings up the subject of benefits.

"I do not have access to the volumes of seal meat that I thought I would," I admit. "But perhaps we can compromise."

He mentions bonbons, chicken nuggets, Rice Krispies treats, and hot dogs.

"You shall have an unlimited supply," I advise him.

We shake hands.

"Come in and let's get started."

He heads toward the front door.

"No, no," I tell him. "I'm grounded for the moment, and if my mother sees me having guests over, she may respond poorly."

So he comes in through the window.

And gets stuck.

And our first meeting is adjourned.

CHAPTER 39

Chin-Ups

I write a letter to Corrina Corrina.

Which I once again encode so it cannot be read by spies.[28]

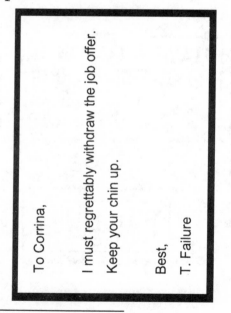

To Corrina,

I must regrettably withdraw the job offer.

Keep your chin up.

Best,
T. Failure

---

[28] It can be read by anyone. Just turn the book on its side. Also, this is getting absurd.

Toody Snooty, So Rude-y

With my agency now fully staffed and operational, I set up a field office at my school.

"What's all this?" asks classmate Nunzio Benedici.

"Read the sign," I say, pointing to the sign on the fence.

"What's the Great Shirt Heist?" he asks.

"Don't you read the newspapers?" I answer.

"I don't," he says.

So I hand him one.

"What's the grits shirt?" he asks.

"Well, well, well," I answer. "Aren't you a little too curious?"

"Huh?"

"You know a lot about this shirt."

"I'm just reading what you handed to me."

"Where were you on the day it was taken?"

"It was taken?"

"Don't get cute with me, Nunzio Benedici. This interrogation can get ugly real fast. Where were you?" I ask again.

"When?"

"Gym class. Tuesday."

"I was at gym."

"Bingo."

"What?"

"You had opportunity," I declare.

"I don't know what that means."

"Do you like shirts?" I ask.

"I guess."

"Well, you wear them, don't you?"

He looks down at his shirt.

"I guess I do," he says.

"Bingo."

"Bingo what?"

"That means you had a motive."

"A motive to do what?"

"I ask the questions here," I tell him.

"I think I'm gonna go back to kickball," he says.

"Fine, I'll free you on your own recognizance."

"What's that?"

"It means you promise to appear at trial."

"What trial?"

"Nunzio Benedici, you're now a suspect in a serious crime. Do you have an attorney?"

"I don't."

"Why not?

"I'm ten."

"That's no excuse," I say. "Now, one more thing."

"Okay, but then I'm gonna play kickball. Recess is almost over."

I walk to the front of the booth and hold out my donation can.

"We here at Failure, Inc., tend to look favorably upon those who contribute to our Recover the Shirt Fund," I tell him.

"No thanks," says Nunzio.

"You're giving nothing?" I ask.

He reaches into his pocket. "Okay, here's a nickel."

I take the nickel from him.

"I shall frame this," I announce. "For these are the first funds earned by Failure, Inc. Care to pose for a celebratory photo?"

"That's okay."

I hear someone on my left clear her throat.

"Have any money left over for the spotted owl?"

"Oh, hi, Toody," says Nunzio.

"How dare you beg for cash from my donors," I admonish her.

"You're the one who set up his booth next to mine."

"I do have some extra money," Nunzio tells her.

"Then give it to me," I tell Nunzio.

"Why should he?" asks Toody.

"Is five dollars good?" Nunzio asks Toody.

"FIVE DOLLARS?" I shout. "That's an outrage. You gave me one nickel!"

"Yes, but I really like animals."

"Well, then give it to me!" I tell him. "I'll buy

food for my polar bear. Polar bears are threatened!"

Nunzio puts the five-dollar bill in Toody's donation box.

"Thank you, Nunzio," says Toody. "Do you have any more?"

"MORE?" I shout. "How greedy can one girl get?"

"Sure," says Nunzio. "I have two more dollars."

"THEN GIVE IT TO ME!" I shout.

"You know what?" says Nunzio. "I have a bunch of friends who like animals, too."

"A POLAR BEAR IS AN ANIMAL!" I yell.

Soon, a large group of kids are surrounding Toody's table.

And when they are gone, Toody's box has more money than I've ever seen in my life.

"Absurd," I mutter.

"It's a very good cause," says Toody.

"So is mine," I declare.

"No, it's not," says Toody. "I heard what you said to him."

"What?"

"That he was a suspect. But if he gave you money, you'd look favorably on him. I think that's called extortion."

"Oh, how rich," I say. "Extortion is your middle name."

"Speaking of which," she says. "My dad was asking what happened to our window."

"So?"

"So gimme that nickel."

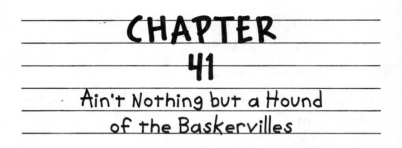

CHAPTER
41

Ain't Nothing but a Hound
of the Baskervilles

After school, I go to the library to see Flo.

Who now has a new sign on his desk.

"Flo," I tell the city librarian. "We have an emergency on our hands."

"We certainly do," says Flo. "You haven't returned the books I gave you."

"Not that. Something bigger."

"I doubt that."

"My detective agency is trying to solve the biggest case this city has ever seen. The Great Shirt Heist. I suspect you've heard of it."

"Nope," he says, not looking up from his book.

"Goodness," I say, "Doesn't anyone in this town read newspapers?"

"I'm the librarian. I read them all."

"Well, not the right ones," I tell him, handing him the latest edition of the *Timmy Times*.

"Sounds important," says Flo.

"Yes," I answer. "And time is critical. Which is why I have my associate canvassing the neighborhood for info.

"But I need more intel," I tell him.

"Intel on what?"

"Names of everyone in this town who has committed a serious crime."

"I see," he says.

But as he says it, someone in the library talks too loud.

And Flo speaks into the library's intercom mic.

"Hello, patrons. Flo here with the Thought of the Day. Loudness makes me unhappy."

Instantly, the library is silent.

Flo turns back to me.

"You were saying?"

"Names," I whisper in the quietist voice I have ever whispered anything. "I need names."

"Come with me," he says.

I follow him through the library until we get to a table upstairs in the back. At which an old woman is reading a book on embroidery patterns.

"Got a minute, Vivian?" he asks.

"Hello, Flo," she answers. "Who's your friend?"

"I'm Timmy Failure," I answer. "I'm looking for known felons. And Flo here has led me right to you."

Flo shakes his head.

"Vivian, tell Timmy here what book you asked me for today."

"*Hound of the Baskervilles,*" she says.

"And what did I say?" asks Flo.

"That somebody didn't bring it back," she answers.

Flo nods. "Timmy, why don't you have a little chat with Vivian."

He pulls out a chair for me, and leaves.

It is now just me and the felon, who looks up from her book on embroidery.

"Everything you say here will be confidential," I advise her.

She doesn't respond.

"You have a right to an attorney."

She doesn't demand one.

"The crime you committed," I tell her. "What was it?"

"I didn't commit any crimes," she answers.

"My colleague Flo says otherwise. And he knows the criminal underworld pretty well."

"Well, I don't know what he's talking about. Who are you again?"

"Timmy Failure, ma'am."

"Okay. And why are you asking me questions?"

"I'm a detective." I hand her my card.

FAILURE INC.
(NOT AS BAD AS IT SOUNDS)

"Well, you're talking to the wrong person," she says. "I've never committed any crimes at all."

"No interactions with the police whatso-ever?"

She thinks for a moment.

"Well, I got a parking ticket once. The meter expired."

"Bingo," I answer. "Why didn't you say that in the first place?"

"Because it was nothing, really," she says.

"I'll be the judge of that," I say. "How much time did you do?"

"I think the meter was for an hour."

"Not the meter, Vivian. Time in the joint."

"Joint?"

"Can."

"Can?"

"Clink."

"Clink?"

"Cooler."

"Cooler?"

"Prison, Viv. Prison."

"Ohhhh. Goodness me. I've never been in prison."

I shake my head.

"Okay, Vivian. You want to do this the hard

way? We'll do it the hard way. I'll need to see some ID."

"This is all very silly," she says. "But fine."

She opens her wallet and flips through the plastic inserts for her driver's license.

I see a photo of grandchildren, a photo of an old man, a photo of a springer spaniel.

And a photo of this:

I now see I am in a grave situation.

With a felon who may be armed.

"Vivian," I say in the calmest voice I can muster. "Promise me you'll stay right here."

"Okay," she says. "Can I read my book on embroidery?"

"Sure," I answer. "Just keep your hands above the table. Where they can be seen."

"Right-o," she says. "They'll just be holding the book."

I nod.

And run for backup.

CHAPTER 42

The Great Grandma Escape

By the time Total and I arrive back at the library, felonious Vivian has escaped.

Most likely via the library roof.

Where she met a waiting helicopter.

SUCKERS.

"I should have tied her down," I tell my polar bear.

He nods.

"That's the thing with hardened felons like Vivian," I say. "They're crafty."

I shake my head.

"And to think she gave me her word."

We leave the library, disgusted with the duplicitous nature of criminals.

I ask my bear if his canvassing of the neighborhood has produced any leads in the Great Shirt Heist.

He reports back that almost every citizen in the town wears shirts.

"That's a broad pool of suspects," I tell him.

And as I say it, we are joined by another citizen wearing a shirt.

"Rollo Tookus, what are you doing here?"

"I need a book I can't get at school," Rollo says. "And what are you doing here?"

"We had an incident with a felon and a helicopter."

"I meant what are you doing out? I thought your mom grounded you again."

"We've been through this before, Rollo."

"Oh, right. She doesn't know."

Rollo shakes his head.

"You take too many risks, Timmy."

"Yes," I answer. "I'm a detective."

"If my mom grounded me, I'd be too scared to even move," says Rollo.

"And that's why you're not a detective."

"Yes," says Rollo. "That's why I'm a big nothing and you're the greatest detective in the history of the world. I wish I was you." [29]

"Thanks."

"Well, I guess I better go get my book."

"Yes, well, before you do," I tell him, "I need your help with something."

---

[29] Language in bold never uttered. —Rollo

"I really have to get that book."

"Rollo, don't worry about a silly book. I can get that for you anytime. I have big connections at the library."

"You do?"

"Of course. And besides, what I need you to do won't take long."

"What is it?"

"It's not wise to discuss it here," I tell him.

CHAPTER
43
Some Girl

With both Vivian and Nunzio loose on the streets, I know I am not safe. So Total, Rollo, and I get to our destination via the city's underground sewer system.[30]

And when we arrive, Rollo immediately has questions.

"Are we getting our hair done or something?"

---

[30] We took the subway.

"Rollo Tookus, I've told you before, information is dangerous. So everything will be on a need-to-know basis."

"Well, I need to know why we're getting our hair done."

"Wrong. All you need to know is what I'm about to tell you."

I pause and search the street for assassins. Seeing none, I continue.

"This is an intelligence gathering site."

"It's a hair and nail salon."

"Right," I answer. "To an amateur, that's what it looks like."

"Because that's what it is."

"You're going to go in there and tell them you want your toes drowned."

"My what?"

"I don't really know. It's what they do."

"Why do I have to do it?"

"Because for reasons I can't yet fathom, my relationship with them has become adversarial. Which is strange, because we're in the same line of work."

"So you've started cutting hair?"

I ignore him.

"Once inside, you're to establish a rapport with the agents," I explain to Rollo. "Make them think you're on their side. Once you've earned their trust, you're to casually inquire about a set of missing books."

"What books?"

"That information is confidential."

"Then how am I supposed to ask for them?"

"Fine. If you must know, they're books on Sherlock Holmes. But that info goes nowhere else."

"Fine."

Rollo walks into the building.

I turn toward Total. "Perhaps you and I should head to a bar to discuss the intelligence you've gathered. This mission will take Rollo at least six hours."

Rollo walks out of the building.

"Some girl has them."

CHAPTER
44
Laps in Judgment

The news that the books have been stolen by an unknown girl is unexpected and profound.

"What is happening to this world?" I ask my polar bear. "First the Great Shirt Heist. Now this."

I shake my head in disgust.

"It seems as though the whole world is one big criminal enterprise," I add. "And all that is stopping them is you and I."

And Rollo.

Sort of.

For I have asked him to distribute a questionnaire to every person in our school who meets the description of the suspect.

Which so far is:

"Timmy, that's half the people in this school," complains Rollo.

"Yes, well, you're the one who got the incomplete description," I answer, and hand him the stack of forms I printed at the library.

And when Rollo meets me in the locker room before P.E., he is carrying only three completed forms.

"That's it?" I ask.

"Yeah. No one wanted to fill them out."

"Let me see one."

He hands me a completed form.

"Who filled this one out?" I ask Rollo.

"Toody," he says. "Her name's at the top."

I examine the form.

NAME: *Toody Tululu*

DID YOU STEAL A SET OF BOOKS FROM
BECKY'S HAIR AND NAIL SALON?
(Please circle your answer)

YES   (NO)

IF YES, WHY HAVE YOU CHOSEN A LIFE
OF CRIME?

*I haven't, but the
spotted owl would like
twenty more dollars.* ☺

"My God, the depravity," I utter under my breath. "The girl will stop at nothing."

"Huh?" asks Rollo.

"Nothing," I answer. "Where's the next one?"

He hands it to me.

NAME: *Corrina Corrina*

DID YOU STEAL A SET OF BOOKS FROM BECKY'S HAIR AND NAIL SALON?
(Please circle your answer)

YES   (NO)

IF YES, WHY HAVE YOU CHOSEN A LIFE OF CRIME?

Not applicable

_____

_____

"What the—?" I say, staring at the name on the form. "She doesn't go to our school."

"I think her family moved and she just got

transferred here," says Rollo. "Why, do you know her?"

"Rollo, she's the girl I was sending messages to!"

"Oh, right."

"You delivered one of them!"

He looks in his gym locker.

"Oh, this thing?" he says, pulling out a sealed envelope.

"You never delivered it?" I cry.

"I tried, but Toody said she didn't want it."

"Rollo Tookus, you're fired!"

"I don't work for you," he says.

"Dodgeball in two minutes!" yells Mr. Beefton, waddling into the locker room in his flip-flops. "If you're late, you're doing twenty laps around the school."

"We better hurry," says Rollo. "We can't be late."

"Relax," I tell him. "I'm keeping an eye on the clock. Where's the last form?"

"Here," he says, handing it to me.

And it is the most mysterious document I have ever held.

NAME: _Can't say_

DID YOU STEAL A SET OF BOOKS FROM BECKY'S HAIR AND NAIL SALON?
(Please circle your answer)

(YES)   NO

IF YES, WHY HAVE YOU CHOSEN A LIFE OF CRIME?

I LOVE YOU,
TIMMY FAILURE !!!
♡♡♡ ♡♡ ♡ ♡ ♡ ♡♡☺

"My God," I declare. "It's a detailed confession. Who gave this to you?"

"I don't know," says Rollo. "Someone just slid it into my locker."

"Of course. They delivered it in the dead of night. Perhaps the school will have surveillance footage."

"We have to go, Timmy."

"Rollo Tookus, where are your priorities? We could be looking at a major break in the investigation."

"Fine. But I don't want to be late. Because I really hate running laps."

"We won't be late," I assure him. "As long as you're keeping track of the time."

"I thought you were keeping tracking of the time," he says.

But I wasn't.

Back at the office, Total and I begin analyzing the evidence we now have.

But it's hard to focus.

Because we can barely move.

"These conditions are inhumane," I cry.

For the "temporary" arrangement with Philippe's car has become more than temporary.

"What kind of person goes on vacation and asks if he can leave his car in your garage for a few days?" I ask Total. "And what kind of mother allows that?"

But we know we must focus.

So I return to the cases.

"Okay, we've had two things stolen in a short amount of time. The books and the shirt. That shows a pattern of criminal conduct."

Total grunts.

"Both were extremely valuable and could fetch a large amount of cash on the black market. That shows a motive."

Total grunts again.

"And both were stolen in the bright light of day. Which shows a level of arrogance bordering on recklessness."

Total nods.

"So it is highly likely that both crimes were committed by the same person."

I turn toward Total.

"And it is also likely that there are witnesses."

My large brain begins working faster and faster.

"But whoever has that information is not just going to voluntarily give it to us. We have to offer them an inducement."

Total stares at me, confused.

"That just means we give them something they want. Cash, diamonds, ponies. It can be anything. The point is to get them talking."

Total nods.

"So here's what I propose," I say, pausing for dramatic effect. "Figs.

"Everyone likes figs. And best of all, they're free. Because a neighbor down the block has a tree. And I believe all trees are public property."

Total grunts.

"And if that doesn't work, we'll go to Phase Two of my plan. And that is to offer them something even better. Combs.

"Think about it," I say. "Everyone has hair. Or at least knows someone who does. People will be telling us everything they know just to get those combs."

Total nods.

"And all of this is in addition to the fact that people already have an innate desire to report wrongdoing simply because it's the right thing to do."

Total is so pleased by this brilliant plan that he raises his arms in celebration.

And hits a storage shelf.

Causing a hammer to fall.

Onto the hood of Philippe's car.
Making a small scratch.

"We shall deny that," I say.

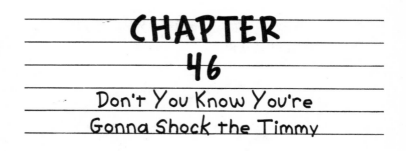

Don't You Know You're
Gonna Shock the Timmy

I proceed to school the next day with a boxful of glorious figs.

And at lunch, I proceed to the playground to set up my field office and begin finding witnesses who will provide critical information on my cases.

And there I receive the shock of my life.

CHAPTER
47

The Demon Who Knew
Too Much

It is a jolt so profound that after school, I sprint to the city library to think.

Oblivious to all those I encounter.

And I run upstairs and sit at a back table.
And catch my breath. And focus.

And suddenly it all makes sense.

Corrina Corrina had been seeing my letters all along. And in them I revealed everything:

- The name of my agency
- Our proposed salary structure
- The identity of potential recruits
- My fondness for pitchforks

And she had been carefully taking notes. Planning her own agency.

And when she was ready, she mysteriously "transferred" to our school so she could pilfer all of my clients one by one.

Which she was now doing.

And worse, she was undercutting my financial model:

It was a betrayal so deep as to be almost incomprehensible.

For she was an associate I had groomed. Nurtured from the ground up. Built from nothing.

And now here she was, at my own school, bent on destroying me.

Turning all the tools I had given her against me.

It was a reversal so profound as to be almost dizzying.

So much so that I didn't even see the person next to me.

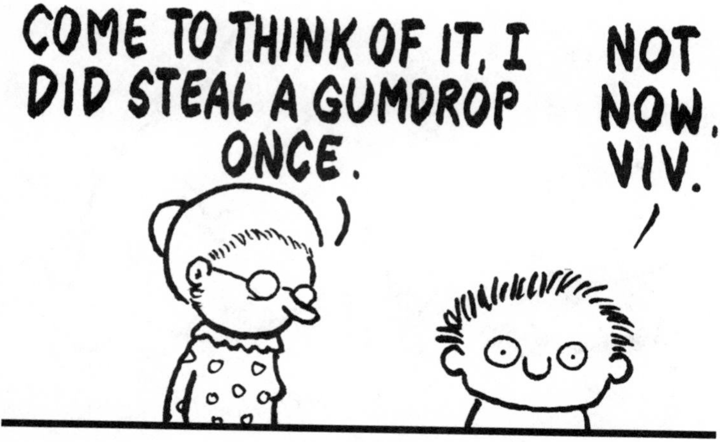
COME TO THINK OF IT, I DID STEAL A GUMDROP ONCE.
NOT NOW, VIV.

I'm Found in the Supermarket

After the library, I summon my polar bear and together we race to the grocery store.

"We will buy all the combs they have," I announce to Total. "And we will hand them out to every man, woman, and child at school. And they will talk. And when they do, we will solve the Great Shirt Heist."

I stop at the front doors of the grocery store and turn back to Total.

"And when we solve it," I add, "our agency will be the most famous in the state, perhaps the nation. And seeing she can't compete, Corrina Corrina will quit. And her agency will be kaput."

My polar bear grunts in agreement.

"Now you wait outside and guard against any potential assassins," I tell him. "I'll be right back."

And so I march into the grocery store.

Looking for an aisle marked Combs.

But instead I find one useless section after another, like Produce, Pasta, and Pet Products.

And Wine.

Where I run into a whiner.

"What are you doing here?" I ask.

"What are *you* doing here?" answers Philippe.

"You're supposed to be on vacation."

"I was. But now I'm back."

He stares at me with suspicious eyes. And flushed with the shock of Corrina's betrayal, I panic.

"I know not what has happened to thy car!"

"Huh?" he says.

"Your car. I knoweth nothing."

"What happened to my car?" he asks.

"Don't ask me," I answer. "For I know not."

"No, really," he says. "What are you talking about?"

"I do not know," I tell him. "For I have experienced a shock so jarring that I believe I have gone mad."

And seeing insanity as my only defense, I leap into the yogurt section.

"Tim, I want to know what happened to my car," he says.

So I climb out of the yogurt section.
And do what I must.
Flee.

When Philippe found out about his car, he talked to my mother about the conversation we had at the grocery store.

And while he thought the important part was his car, she honed in on something entirely different.

"You went to the grocery store when I specifically said you were grounded."

I ponder once again using insanity as a defense.

But I know my mother doesn't care.

And there is no yogurt.

So I surrender.

"Mistakes were made," I admit.

"What is it with you lately, Timmy? Breaking your promises. Breaking the wall."

"I did not break that window," I respond.

"I didn't say 'window.'"

"Oh."

"Why?"

"No reason."

"Oh, Timmy," she mutters.

And drops her head into her hands.

And I crumble like a captured spy.

"Okay. I was sending a note to Toody and I accidentally broke her window."

"Timmy, no."

"It was an accident. I swear."

"Oh, my God, Timmy. What is going on with you?"

"I don't know," I answer.

"You are going to have to tell Toody's dad what you did. And you are going to have to pay for it. I don't care if it takes you saving up all the allowances you make between now and college."

"I know," I say.

"That means doing all the chores I give you."

"I know," I answer. "And I think I know right where to start."

CHAPTER
50
Garage Banned

I spend that evening making the garage as neat and orderly as I can.

Finding a place for every box.

Until there is no more office.

"Well, this is the cleanest I've ever seen this place," says my mother as she walks into the garage.

She looks at the clear area where I'm standing.

"What happened to your office?"

"I got rid of it," I answer. "It was just in the way. And besides, this way, nothing can fall on Philippe's car."

She smiles.

"I'll tell you, Timmy. If that was a scratch, it was about the smallest scratch I've ever seen."

I go back to my boxes.

"Where should I put this thing?" I say.

"Since he's not coming back," I add.

"Bring it over here," says my mother.

I set it on the ground beside her.

She sits down on the garage floor beside me.

"Do you want to talk about anything?" she asks.

"Negative," I answer.

We both stare at the box.

"Do you think there's a monkey in it?" I ask.

"Negative," she answers.

"Flame thrower?" I ask.

"Probably not."

"Rocket launcher?" I ask.

"Timmy, if you're so curious, why don't you just look?" she says.

"Is that okay?"

"I don't see why not."

"Okay," I tell her. "But stand back. In case it explodes."

I undo the tape on the box and slowly open the cardboard flaps.

But it doesn't explode.

"It's just a bunch of dumb papers."

I keep looking through the box.

"And this stupid thing."

My mom smiles. "That's a scarf he used to wear," she says.

"Great. A bunch of papers and a stupid scarf. What a waste of time this has been."

"Well, at least nothing exploded."

"True. Though I'd rather have a flame thrower."

I stare at the scarf.

"You said he wore this?" I ask.

"Every day."

"Why?" I ask.

"I think he thought it made him look sophisticated."

"Did it?"

"Yeah," she says, laughing. "I suppose. Why? Do you want to wear it?"

"Never," I answer.

"Well, then let's pack all this back up."

So we repack the box.

"So what are you going to do about an

office now?" she asks as she lifts the box onto a shelf.

"I don't know," I answer. "Not sure if it matters."

"Oh, a detective has to have an office."

I shrug.

"I might have an idea," she says.

CHAPTER
51

Clothes Encounters

"Mother, your room exploded," I say.

"It didn't explode," she says. "I just put some of my clothes on the bed."

"What for?"

"To make a little room in my closet."

"For what?"

"Open the closet door," she says.
So I open it.

"What's all this?" I ask.

"I thought it could be your office."

"But what about your clothes and stuff?"

"I can find some other place to put all that."
She smiles.

"So," she says, "will it do?"

I walk into the office and look around.

"Well, I have a polar bear now. He's my employee."

"Interesting," she says.

"So he'll need his own cubicle."

"I suppose we can find space," she says. "Is he large?"

"Fifteen hundred pounds. Give or take."

"Oh, that is rather large. I might have to move a few more dresses."

"And I'll have to change the sign," I add. "The name of the agency is Failure, Inc."

"Ah, yes," she says. "I wasn't sure. But that can be easily changed."

"And I was hoping for an indoor pool," I add. "You know, so I can swim laps at lunch."

"Of course."

"And a minibar," I add.

"No minibar," she answers.

I glance back at my mother.

"Well?" she asks. "What do you think?"

So I answer.

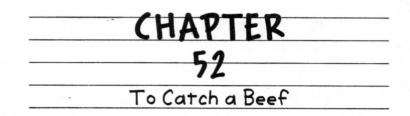

CHAPTER 52

To Catch a Beef

With prestigious office space now secured, I march triumphantly to school with my employee.

"We do not have combs," I announce to my polar bear. "But we have more genius than the world has ever seen."

And more importantly, we have a plan.

And when I give the prearranged signal, Total breaks off and heads toward Becky's Hair and Nail Salon to watch for any suspicious comings and goings.

"Keep a detailed log of everyone you see," I advise him.

And I enter the school.

And at P.E., I approach Rollo Tookus.

"I have solved the Great Shirt Heist," I declare.

"You mean the thing with your shirt getting stolen?"

"Of course. Do you not watch the nightly news?"

"I don't," he says.

"This generation is sadly uninformed," I mutter, shaking my head. "Well, be that as it may, I have solved the entire case."

"So what happened?"

"Think for a moment," I tell him. "The shirt was stolen while it was in the locker room and all of our class was in the gym."

"True."

"So it couldn't be any of us."

"Okay."

"But then there's our P.E. teacher, Mr. Beefton."

"Yeah. What about him?"

"Where was he that whole time?" I ask.

"In the gym with us."

"He was?" I ask.

"Yeah. He doesn't leave us by ourselves."

"Right," I say, and pause to think. "But

consider this. P.E. teachers are paid vast sums of money. Millions, in fact."

"I don't think they are."

"You are wrong. I own a business. I know."

"Okay. Even if that was true, so what?"

"So Beefton has the means to hire someone. Like hitmen!"

"I think hitmen kill people," says Rollo.

"Not this time," I explain. "This time they were hired to break into a locker room and steal a priceless shirt."

I shake my head.

"God knows what Beefton paid them," I add. "Probably a hundred grand, minimum."

"You think Beefton paid someone a hundred thousand dollars to steal your grits T-shirt?"

"I don't think, Rollo. I know."

And I clap my hands.

And the police kick open the locker room doors.

And there before us is our P.E. teacher, Mr. Beefton.

In handcuffs.

"I don't know how you solved it," the defeated Beefton says to me. "But you did. And it was brilliant."

Beefton tries to high-five me, but his arms are in shackles.

"You are the best detective in the world," he says. "And a person would be a fool to hire Corrina Corrina instead of you."

"Indeed they would," I answer, and turn coldly toward the cops.

"Take him away."

CHAPTER 53

Last Diversion, We Promise.
And Again, We Are Really
Sorry About the Shoddy
Nature of This Book.

(The following is a transcript of yet another dispute between Timmy and Rollo. We truly regret this entire debacle.   —Editors, Disney-Hyperion)

ROLLO: That's not what happened in the locker room, Timmy.

TIMMY: It is precisely what happened.

ROLLO: No. I was there.

(Sound of door opening. Female voice.)

WOMAN: Timmy, why are you holding a bowling ball?

TIMMY: Mother, it's a bomb.

WOMAN: Oh. Well, Rollo's dad is on the phone. He says dinner is in fifteen minutes.

TIMMY: Tell him twenty.

WOMAN: Nope. Our dinner's almost ready, too. So hurry up.

TIMMY: You're rushing brilliance!

WOMAN: It happens.

(Sound of door closing.)

TIMMY: You heard her, Rollo. We don't have time for your stupid account of what happened in the locker room.

ROLLO: Okay, I'll just add it into the book later.

TIMMY: You will not.

ROLLO: I will.

TIMMY: I expressly forbid it.

ROLLO: Okay, then I'll just take my laptop and go home for dinner.

(Sound of a trash can being kicked. Indecipherable yelling.)

TIMMY: You are a cruel man, Rollo Tookus.

CHAPTER
54

The Chapter Timmy Did Not Want You to See. But Too Bad, Here It Is.

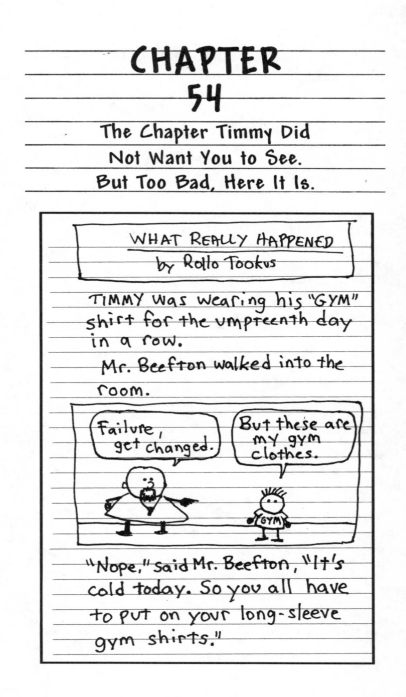

So for the first time in a long time, Timmy took off his "GYM" ~~shirt~~ t-shirt.

And when he did, he discovered something underneath it.

Because on that day back when Timmy was asked to take off his "GRITS" shirt, he did not take off his "GRITS" shirt.

He just put the "GYM" shirt over it.

And forgot.

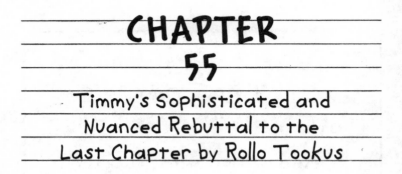

CHAPTER 55

Timmy's Sophisticated and Nuanced Rebuttal to the Last Chapter by Rollo Tookus

LIES
LIES
LIES

CHAPTER
56
Every Fig You Take,
I'll Be Watching You

With the Great Shirt Heist solved and my triumph complete, I use recess to take a well-earned break at my field office.

Where I shake my head at my soon-to-be-failing competitor.

SO SAD TO SEE.

FAILURE
Inc.

When suddenly I hear a familiar voice. "What are you gloating about?"

"Mind you not," I tell Toody Tululu. "For you cannot ruin my day of celebration."

"What are you celebrating?" she asks.

"A glorious triumph," I announce. "For BEHOLD, I have solved the Great Shirt Heist."

"I don't know what that is," she says.

"Doesn't anyone here read newspapers?" I ask.

"No," she replies. "But I do know about the spotted owl. And I don't believe you've—"

"HA!" I cut her off. "You shall no longer extort me for cash, Toody Tululu."

"Well, then I guess I'll just tell your mom you were out when you were grounded."

"Negative. She already knows."

"She knows?"

"Yes."

"Well, then I'll tell her about the window."

"Negative. She already knows that also."

"What? How did she find out?"

"I told her. For I am an honest and upright citizen."

"Interesting," she says. "I wonder if Mr. Chikini thinks that."

"Who's Mr. Chikini?" I ask.

"The neighbor whose figs you stole."

"I deny everything."

"I knew you were gonna say that," she says. "So I took a photo."

"And don't try to rip it up," she says. "Because I made copies."

She holds out her donation box. "A hundred dollars should do."

Total Shakedown

At home in my new office that afternoon, I put the dreaded Toody Tululu out of my mind and celebrate the solving of the Great Shirt Heist with my loyal polar bear.

"We have solved the biggest case of our gen-eration," I tell him. "Take whatever is in the petty cash drawer and buy the most expensive champagne in the world.[31] For we are at the peak of our profession."

I raise my arms in triumph.

Total nods and slides a piece of paper across my desk.

"What's this?" I ask. "A thank-you note for the opportunities I've provided you?"

But I read it.

And it is not that.

---

[31] The most expensive champagne in the world costs $49,000 a bottle. Timmy did not buy it.

"What do you mean you want to be a name partner?" I ask. "I'm the only partner in Failure, Inc."

Total slides another note across the table.

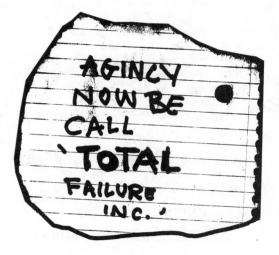

I am stunned by the effrontery.

"While I hate to introduce a foul note in our otherwise glorious day, I must say that your timing is rather uncouth," I tell my polar bear. "Could you at least have waited until the party was over?"

Total shakes his head.

"Well, surely this is negotiable," I add.

He shakes his head and passes me another note.

"Corrina Corrina?" I cry, flabbergasted. "You wouldn't."

But he nods that he would.

And seeing that I have no choice in this

distasteful negotiation, I agree to his outrageous demands.

With a caveat.

"As you are now a name partner in my detective agency, your workload will increase mightily. You will have to show up earlier. Stay later. Work harder. Act smarter. Do you agree to these conditions?"

He nods.

And so I make it official.

CHAPTER
58
Drop Me a Note

"Here is fifty dollars I got from my sock drawer," I tell Flo the Librarian. "I saved it from all my birthdays."

He stares at the money.

"If that is not enough," I add, "I am prepared to go to library jail."

"Why are you handing me money?" he asks.

"For the missing library books. From what I can deduce, I believe Mr. Beefton took them."

"Who's that?"

"P.E. teacher," I answer. "He'll steal the shirt off your back. And he did."

Flo stands.

"You talking about these books?" he asks.

"How did you get them?" I ask.

"Book drop."

"What's that?"

"Big box. Outside. For returning books after hours."

"Did you see who dropped them in there?"

"Oh, yeah," he says. "You might not know this about librarians, but we spend all night on the lawn to see who puts books in the drop box."

"Good work," I answer. "I'll get a police sketch artist in here and you can give him a description."

"Timmy."

"Yes?"

"I have no idea who put them in there," he says. "But if it's any help, this note fell out of one of the books."

"From who?"

"No idea. But I gotta go. Someone upstairs is not using their whisper voice."

I watch as Flo runs off, bounding up the stairs three at a time.

And I read the disturbing note.

Hi:

Found these at Becky's salon.
Have a wonderfuliciously great
day!!!!!!!!!!!!!!!

CHAPTER
59
Study as She Goes

I rush from the library to Rollo's house.

And burst into his room.

"Major developments," I announce. "Stop everything you're doing."

"I have to study," says Rollo.

"That is a grand waste of time, Rollo Tookus."

"No, it's not. I need all A's."

"Detectives do not care about grades."

"Yeah, well I want to go to Stanford one day."

"Stan's Ford? What is that? A used-car dealership?"

"Stanford. It's a university."

"Yeah, well, it sounds like a disreputable sham. And besides, I'm about to break the second major case of my young career. So you might want to listen."

"I'm really busy, Timmy."

"Rollo, this will take no more than three hours."

"Three hours?" he says. "I don't have three hours."

"Sorry, but this is very involved."

"Timmy, I don't even know what you're talking about."

"A note, Rollo. We have a note from the suspect."

"Suspect in what?"

"The Great Book Heist. The case everyone is talking about."

Rollo sighs and puts down his book. "You're not gonna leave until I help you, are you?"

"That's correct."

"Fine. Let me see it."

"All right. But be very careful," I say, handing him the evidence. "You should probably wear gloves."

"You weren't wearing gloves."

"True," I say, pointing at the note. "I also spilled juice on it."

He examines the evidence.

"Just so you know," I tell him, "there will be many steps involved. Handwriting analysts. Fingerprinting. Database queries. We may even have to bring in the Federal Bureau of Investigation."

"It's Molly Moskins."

"And the bureau can take months to chart all the handwriting indicators."

"It's Molly Moskins."

"The risk, of course, is that the FBI will try to shoehorn their way into the case. They have no respect for local jurisdictions."

"It's Molly Moskins."

"And believe me, I don't need any feds breathing down my neck."

"Timmy, I just told you who it was."

"Who?"

"Molly Moskins. She's the only person I know who combines the words 'wonderful' and 'deliciously' and 'great.' Also, you said you left the books in the nail salon, and I know she gets her nails done there. So she probably just saw the books and returned them to the library."

I laugh uproariously.

"No offense," I say, shaking my head. "But you are but an amateur. And whoever this person was went to great lengths to preserve their anonymity."

"Timmy," says Rollo.

"What now?"

"She wrote her name on the back."

"Good God," I reply. "Who is this brazen Molly Moskins?"

"She sits behind you in art class."

"Really?"

"Every day."

"Of course. So she can sneak up behind me and take me out. Probably with a paintbrush."

"I doubt it."

"Because she's a trained assassin."

"Definitely not."

"I wonder if she's employed by the devil."

"Who?"

"Corrina Corrina."

"That new girl? She's nice."

"Wrong. She's trying to destroy me. She started her own detective agency."

"I think she's always had it, Timmy. I think she just loves detective stuff."

"Wrong again. But stay focused, Rollo. Because it looks like I'll have to arrest this Molly girl."

"Whatever, Timmy. But I have to study. So you should probably go home."

"Your small administrative role in solving this case will not be forgotten, Rollo Tookus. Minimal though it was, it was still something."

"Goodbye, Timmy."

Splish Splash I Was
Taking Advantage of
My Employer

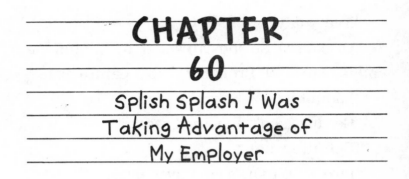

I rush to the office to find my polar bear.

But he is not there.

So I search the house.

And find him here:

"What's all this?" I ask. "It's the middle of the workday."

But he doesn't respond.

"You've just been made a name partner. And this is how you pay me back?"

He offers me a sip of his drink.

"I don't drink on the job," I tell him. "And neither should you."

He sips from his curly straw.

"And by the way, what happened at the nail salon? I specifically stationed you outside of it to watch for any suspicious comings and goings. And now I hear from a civilian that a criminal named Molly Moskins has been frequenting it."

He shrugs his shoulders.

"This is an outrage," I declare. "I changed the name of the agency for you."

I pace back and forth across the bathroom tile.

He turns on the radio and begins rocking back and forth to the music.

"Now you're dancing?" I ask. "Is there no end to your effrontery?"

He turns up the volume of the radio.

I click it off.

"And by the way," I add. "I wasn't going to bring this up, but I showed your résumé to Rollo Tookus, and he said there is no such thing as graduating 'magna suppa duppa.' Do you want to explain that?"

He writes a note on a piece of paper, then tears it off and hands it to me.

"You lied on your résumé? Do you know how serious that is? Sure, it was just about your education, but do you see how that could cast doubt on the employment history you listed?"

He passes me another note.

"You lied about everything?" I shout.

He nods his head vigorously.

"Okay, that does it," I announce. "I am a generous employer, but you've abused my goodwill. Total, you're fired."

But then he feels around on the top of the bathroom counter for another piece of paper.

Which he hands to me.

It is his employment contract.

"What?" I shout. "You can't be fired? Is this legally binding?"

Total nods.

"So you can do whatever you want?"

Total nods. Sips from his straw.

I pace the bathroom floor again.

Until I stumble upon a genius idea.

"Fine. You are not fired. But there is nothing in that contract about your food supply."

Total stops sipping from his drink.

"So until you correct your bad attitude, there will be no chicken nuggets."

He stands aghast.

"And until you get back to work, there will be no hot dogs."

Total drops his curly straw.

"And until you start impressing me, there will be no bonbons."

And before I can say anything else, he has leapt from the tub and sprinted down the hallway.

And is back at work.

A changed bear.

CHAPTER
61
Spotted

Reeling from Total's mendacity, I resolve to reward those who have made positive contributions to the agency.

So I head to a department store to obtain a gift for Rollo Tookus.

"I would like to procure a clothing item for a dear friend," I tell the clerk. "To reward him for his contribution to my agency."

"Give me the nicest item of clothing you have," I tell her. "Cost is of no concern."

She shows me a particularly nice sweater.

"Wrap it up," I tell her. "And throw in five more. And while it is of no import, may I inquire as to the cost?"

She shows me the price tag.

"One hundred dollars!" I exclaim. "I'm being robbed!"

So I hold up my arms like I'm being robbed.

"I need to excuse myself," says the clerk. "I have another customer."

I keep my arms raised as a form of protest.

But cannot help but see the other customer.

"I'd like some hair scrunchies," she tells the clerk. "To hold back my thick, luxurious hair."

The clerk hands her a hair scrunchie.

Which Toody wraps around her hair.

"This looks lovely," says Toody. "I'll take a dozen."

"And how will you be paying?" asks the clerk.

"Cash," she says.

And I watch as she reaches into a box I have seen before.

I walk up to her.

"Are those for the spotted owl?" I ask.

"It's not what it looks like!" she says.

"It looks like you're buying hair scrunchies for spotted owls."

She grabs the money back from the clerk and throws the hair scrunchie on the counter.

"Promise me you won't say anything," she says.

"About how owls wear hair scrunchies?"

"About anything," she says nervously.

"I do not generally discuss owls," I answer. "Spotted or otherwise."

CHAPTER
62
U Is for Ungrateful

Toody is so appreciative of my not discussing the spotted owl's hair scrunchies that she gives me back all of the extortion money.

And I use those funds to purchase a personalized sweatshirt for Rollo.

"Thank you, Timmy!" says Rollo. "Though I think you spelled 'Stanford' wrong."

"Do not look a gift pig in the mouth," I advise him.

"Horse," says Rollo.

"Do not look a horse pig in the mouth."

"No," says Rollo. "The expression is 'Don't look a gift horse in the mouth.'"

But I have no time for grammar.

For I have one last task to perform.

A Segue to the
End of the Book

"Where are you off to?" asks my mother.

"I should be asking you questions," I answer.
"Like what in God's name is that thing?"

"It's a Segway. I won it in a raffle."

"It is dangerous and unstable. Please get off."

"It's fine."

"It's a death trap."

"It's not a death trap, Timmy."

"Oh, to have a mother that is not reckless and crazed," I lament.

"Oh, c'mon, Timmy. Go for a ride with me."

"Mother, I would not a ride a vehicle like that for all the tea and china."

"Tea *in* China."

"You are the second person to try to correct my grammar in the last hour. It is very annoying. Especially given the fact that my grammar is never wrongly."

She says nothing.

"Well, so long," I tell my mother, "I must be going."

"You never said where."

"Official detective business."

"Foreign or domestic?" she asks.

"Domestic."

"Ah," she says, "Then where's your grits shirt?"

"It is no longer my agency's motto. For I have decided to change it."

"To what?"

"Greatness. It has the same *gr* sound as *grits,* but with a bit more oomph."

"I like it," she says. "But you're no longer wearing anything distinctive."

"Let me worry about that, Mother."

"Timmy, you are not taking that pipe."

"I am not."

"I'm serious, Timmy."

"I know, Mother," I answer. "And please be careful on that vehicle. I'd like to have a mother when I get back."

"Love you," she says, in public, out loud, where it can be heard by anyone.

I shake my head at her indiscretion.

And stand upon my toes to whisper into her ear.

"Mother."

"Yes?"

"Your son feels the same."

CHAPTER 64
Arrest Development

With an address provided to me by Rollo, I walk the gritty streets toward my destination.

Wary of the immoral underbelly of the big city.

But knowing it's the job I signed up for.

So I maintain a jaded eye, sensitive to any sudden movements, but hardened to the cruel reality of the urban landscape.

Until I arrive at the designated address.

And pound on the front door.

And spot the dame.

"Timmy!" says Molly Moskins.

"Hello," I answer.

"That scarf looks very good on you," she says.

"Yes. It's quite distinctive," I answer.

"Where'd you get it?" she asks.

"It belonged to my father. And please, no more personal questions."

"Okay. Do you want to come in?"

"Afraid not, Molly. But I need you to come with me."

"Sure!" she says. "Are you taking me somewhere fun?"

"Federal prison."

"How exciting!"

"For the theft of books from Becky's Hair and Nail Salon. A Class One felony."

"Let's go!"

I take her by the hand and begin walking with her.

"Is the prison far away?" she asks as we descend down her front steps.

"A mile or so," I answer.

"Will you be walking me the whole way?"

"Of course," I answer. "You're a considerable flight risk."

"I really am!" she says. "So whatever you do, don't let go of my hand!"

We begin walking down the rough and dirty streets.

"Should we stop somewhere for a quiet dinner?" she asks.

"No more questions, Molly Moskins."

"Timmy?"

"I said no more questions, Molly."

"Just one more."

"Okay, what?" I answer.

"Can you arrest me every day?"

THE
END

CHAPTER
65

Not Sure What's Going On, Because Timmy Already Wrote "The End" and Usually There's Nothing After That in a Book

And then I won the Nobel Prize.[32]

For Greatness.[33]

---

[32] He did not.

[33] No such award.

THE
END

CHAPTER 66

Now the Book Should Definitely Be Over Because He's Written "The End" Twice, but No, We're Still Here.

I forgot to say that I defused the bomb.[34]

And saved all of humanity.[35]

---

[34] Bowling ball.

[35] I can't take any more of this. I'm going home to eat dinner.
—Rollo

THE
END

CHAPTER
67

WE GIVE UP.

Okay, this really is the end.

THE
END

GO HOME NOW.

STEPHAN PASTIS is the creator of *Pearls Before Swine,* an acclaimed comic strip that appears in more than eight hundred US newspapers. Stephan took an unusual route to becoming a best-selling comics creator: He went to law school. Hopelessly bored sitting in class at UCLA, he found himself sketching the character Rat. Creative inspiration followed him through graduation in 1993 to his first law firm job in San Francisco, and *Pearls Before Swine* was born in 2002. In 2013, Pastis was inspired to break out of the comic-strip box, penning his first children's book, *Timmy Failure: Mistakes Were Made,* which became an instant *New York Times* best seller. *Mistakes Were Made* was quickly followed by six other installments in the popular middle-grade series starring a brilliantly bad detective with a polar bear sidekick. Stephan lives in Northern California.